WOEFUL WEDDING DAY

Jamie Blair

Cover Design by Kelly York at Sleepy Fox Studio

Created with Vellum

1

Wedding bells chimed, reverberating through Metamora. Or maybe those were tornado sirens. Summer in Indiana meant spending a lot of time in the basement.

"Take shelter," Carl Finch--my soon-to-be step-dad--called out. "Follow me downstairs."

My mom moved in with Carl when they got engaged six months ago. His house was actually a modern day castle that sat atop the highest hill in Metamora, hence its name, Hilltop Castle.

"Let me just grab my wedding planner and thank you cards," Mom said, darting around the great room. "Those can't get blown away." My mother was the stereotypical Bridezilla, and had been stomping around town in a moody frenzy of wedding planning for weeks. The fact that she'd done all of this before over forty years ago didn't matter. This wedding would be her dream wedding, and a tornado was no match for a bride on a mission. "Cameron," she shouted to me, "grab that box of photo frames. Oh! Monica, my heels! I can't go down the aisle barefoot even if it's because a tornado ripped through town."

My sister, half way to the basement door, looked back at me shell shocked. Monica wasn't willing to risk her life to rescue a pair of heels. "I'll buy you another pair, mom," she said. "Come on!"

"Angela!" Carl shouted from the bottom of the staircase located behind a giant wooden door that had to have taken ten body builders to bring inside the house. "Hurry, dear! The weather station is saying we're right in the path of a funnel cloud!" A loud crack of thunder emphasized his anxiety.

The three of us hustled by a suit of armor in the hallway, our arms loaded with wedding paraphernalia, and lumbered down the steps. I'd never been in the basement of Hilltop Castle, and this was like no other basement I'd ever seen in my life. Instead of the historically accurate castle dungeon, I stepped into a medieval tavern with heavy wooden tables and chairs, barrels of ale, wrought iron chandeliers and sconces with candles. There were even pendants with crests hanging from the ceiling.

"Wow," Monica breathed, her head thrown back to take it all in.

"This is like walking back in time," I said, "I think I hear a lute playing."

"That's still the sirens," Mom said, dropping her planner on a table. She'd never been afraid of tornado warnings. Me, on the other hand, I was keeping my mind busy so I didn't dart behind the ornately carved bar, curl into the fetal position and whimper.

Quickly, I balanced the box of mini photo frames on one hip and yanked my phone from my jacket pocket to send a text to my husband, Ben, and step-daughter, Mia, telling them to take shelter and send me a message to let me know they were safe.

"I'll take those," Carl said, relieving me of the box. Each wedding guest would have their photo taken and the engraved frames would forever remind the recipient of Carl and Angela's anniversary date. I knew my mother, and she'd expect a card or phone call from each and every one of them since they had no excuse to not remember.

"Don't worry, ladies," Carl said, setting the box down and rounding the bar, "this house has never had one bit of storm damage. I doubt today will be the day it does."

If I lived in a tall castle on the highest spot in town I wouldn't be quick to make that wager. It seemed to me that we were sitting at the bottom of a giant lightening rod. If the tornado hit, the roof would lift off into space and take the suit of armor with it like an astronaut flying into orbit wearing a tin can.

"I'm not worried about the house," Mom said. "I'm worried about the church. What if it's flooded tomorrow?"

Like all of the older Metamorans, Carl had an attachment to the old church in town next to the canal, Metamora Faith and Friends, that was no longer used for services due to the number of times it had been flooded. Much to my mother's chagrin, he'd insisted on having their wedding there tomorrow, so the threat of needing rafts and inter tubes for the guests was real.

"It'll all work out," Carl told her. "Here, have a glass of wine and relax. Take this downtime and enjoy it." He handed her a glass of red wine.

"I can't enjoy it. I have too much to do. Too much to worry about. Cecelia was supposed to be here hours ago. I hope she's not driving in this storm."

Mom's roommate from college was a wedding planner to the rich and willing to spend tens of thousands of dollars on a wedding in Los Angeles. I'd met Cecelia once when I was a kid. All I remember of her is a mane of red hair and long red nails, and red lipstick on a loud, boisterous woman who smoked long, thin cigarettes.

"I'm sure she's fine, dear," Carl said.

"This is going to be a long twenty-four hours," Monica whispered, leaning into me.

"I'm just glad I wasn't around for the first wedding."

Monica grinned. "Speaking of Dad. Did you know--"

"What are you two whispering about?" Mom asked, giving us her squinty eyed gaze which was half warning and half suspicion.

"Nothing," both of us replied in unison.

"You're finishing that thought later," I muttered to Monica under my breath.

"Oh, there's that cat again!" Mom jumped up from her chair,

pointing to a bookshelf in the corner. "How is he getting in all the time?"

"He's harmless," I said. It was Spook, the cat who seemed to have secret portals inside everyone's house in town. He showed up and left when he felt the urge.

"I don't want him in this house," she said. "Next thing you know we'll have to flea bomb."

"He's never brought in fleas," Carl said, reaching over and patting Mom's hand. "He's been around for years, and I've never seen even one."

Bless Carl Finch. I don't know how he was spending every day and night with Mom in her current state of heightened mean and crazy, but he hadn't lost his cool even once. I was certain though that just like the rest of us, he'd be breathing a sigh of relief when tomorrow's festivities were over and she was back to her normal self--only slightly annoying and sometimes irrational.

A procession of trumpets sounded from upstairs. "Someone's at the door," Carl said.

Nothing like having a royal pronouncement that you rang the doorbell.

"Cecelia!" Mom jumped up and high tailed it for the stairs.

"Now, let me answer it," Carl called, dashing after her. "You never know who could be out there in this storm."

Monica and I followed them upstairs. Whoever it was had to be soaked to the bone. Even an umbrella wouldn't be a match for the wind and rain. Carl opened the door a crack. "It's a young woman," he said, throwing it open all the way. The sirens blared louder, rushing in on the wind. "Come inside. What can we do for you?"

"What on earth are you doing out in this?" Mom asked.

"Is Cecelia here?" the twenty-something girl asked. "I'm Grace, her assistant."

"Grace!" Mom hustled her further inside. "Monica, grab her a towel from the bathroom, please."

"We haven't heard from Cecelia yet," Carl said.

"She flew in early this morning," Grace told us. "She rented a car. It's only about an hour and a half drive from Indianapolis."

"She's staying at The Briar Bird Inn," Mom said. "I've called and checked with Judy several times today and she's not there."

"Let me call again," Carl said, taking his cell phone out of his pocket.

"When was the last time you heard from her?" I asked.

"She sent me a text when she landed at the airport," Grace said. "That was at ten this morning. She told me to call her when I got to town. I know she was planning on spending some time with you catching up, Ms. Cripps-Zaborowski, so I took a later flight since she wouldn't need me."

It was seven PM, so nine hours had passed since Grace heard from Cecelia. What could she have gotten herself into in nine hours between here and Indianapolis?

"I expected her around noon," Mom said, ushering her into the living room. Monica came back with a towel and handed it to Grace.

"Judy hasn't heard from her," Carl said, striding into the room. "Can I get you something? Tea? Wine? Brandy?"

"Water?" I threw out. Not everyone was keen on after dinner spirits. Speaking of dinner... "Have you eaten? I can get you something."

"I'm fine," she said. "Thank you."

We all sat down, doing our best to ignore the threat of a tornado, and focusing on the missing wedding planner.

"Maybe she decided to stay somewhere else," Monica said. "I'll call around and check with Cass at Fiddle Dee Doo Inn and a few others nearby."

"Thank you, Monica," Mom said giving her a gracious smile.

"I can let Ben know to look out for her," I offered.

Mom frowned. "I don't think we need to call the cops yet, Cameron."

I shrugged and sank farther into the couch cushions.

"I'm sure she's fine," Carl said. "She probably heard the weather report and decided to pull over somewhere. Maybe she's still in Indianapolis."

"She always answers her calls and texts right away," Grace said. "She even sleeps with her phone. It's one of the reasons her clients love her so much."

"Let's not worry," Carl said. "I'm sure there's an explanation."

Grace patted her long, honey blond hair with the towel. She'd left her flats at the door and I noticed the pink sparkly nail polish on her toes didn't match her lavender fingernails that looked chipped. She'd probably been biting them in worry over Cecelia. She was thin and tan and very much the California girl next door.

"She's been through so much lately," Grace said. "And she's so fragile. Her health hasn't been the best. It's all the stress. I keep telling her I'll take on more responsibility, but she's so dedicated to her clients that she gives them all of her energy and attention."

Fragile? That's not how I remembered Cecelia, of course it had been a few decades and the memories from being a kid weren't always reliable. She'd be in her sixties now, like Mom, and even if that wasn't exactly old, if her health wasn't the best, I could see why Grace would worry.

Monica came back in the living room. "Nobody else has a Cecelia Evans registered as a guest."

"When this storm lets up we'll go out and see if we can find her," Carl said. "I'm sure she's fine." He sat next to mom and put an arm around her shoulders.

My phone rang and the display read, Ben. "Hi," I said, answering. "Where are you?"

"Mia and I are home safe," he said. "I picked her up from work at the Soda Pop Shop. They closed early since the canal's flooding and nobody's out to buy candy."

"The canal's flooding?" I whispered. Lord love a duck. Mom would have the fit of all fits if she had to wear a bathing suit and swim down the aisle.

"It is. It's not across the street yet, so our house is okay, and it wouldn't have reached the church yet, so all is still well on that front."

"We're missing mom's friend, the wedding planner," I said.

"What do you mean missing?"

"She was supposed to be here around noon. Her assistant just showed up and she hasn't heard from her either."

"After the storm we'll go look for her. I'm sure she's waiting it out somewhere safe."

"I'm sure she is," I said. We ended our call, and even though Ben was a police officer and had been through a ton of missing person false alarms, an ominous feeling had settled into my spine making it tingle. The woman who slept with her phone wouldn't have turned it off while traveling, and not during a tornado warning, and especially not when her friend and client was expecting her to arrive today, one day before the wedding.

No, something wasn't right with this situation. I could only hope it would turn out all right and help keep the bride from a state of hysteria.

2

Carl's phone rang.

"Is nobody aware that there's a storm going on?" Mom asked, becoming irritated. "Unless that's Cecelia or someone who knows where she is, they should be sheltering in place and not calling people."

Carl turned away with his phone to his ear. The call was short. He hung up and turned, making desperate eye contact with me and Monica. Unfortunately, Mom caught on to his silent plea before we could do anything to help.

"What is it, Carl?" she asked. "It's something bad, I can tell. Is it about Cecelia?"

"No, no, nothing like that." He pocketed his phone and forced a smile onto his lips. "Reverend Stroup has laryngitis and no voice. He's called in Pastor Sonya from the new church to officiate the wedding tomorrow."

"I don't know Pastor Sonya," Mom said. "Do you know Pastor Sonya? Does anyone in this room know Pastor Sonya?" Her voice rose to a shrill, panicked octave. We were moments from full on hysteria.

"I've met her," Monica said, smiling and nodding like a giddy crazy lady trying to keep Mom from flipping out. "She's really nice.

She comes in with her niece to visit with the rescue dogs the Brookville Shelter volunteers bring in every month."

"That's not a glowing review of her pastoral abilities, Monica," Mom said between clenched teeth. "She could have twenty dogs in fancy dresses and it still wouldn't tell me if I wanted the woman to preside over my wedding."

"Cass loves her," I said. "She goes to the new church and I've heard her talk about how wonderful Pastor Sonya is a lot of times."

It was mostly true. Cass did go to the new church and she had mentioned Pastor Sonya, the rest I embellished, but it was for a good cause.

"Stewart and Irene attend church there, too," Carl added. "I haven't heard any bad reports, and you know Irene would make sure the entire town knew if Pastor Sonya wasn't any good."

"True," Mom said. "Irene does love to throw her influence around."

I had no idea my in-laws attended the new church, which didn't speak volumes for Irene's approval, because she would have thrown her influence my way to make sure Ben, Mia, and I were there on Sunday mornings. I kept meaning to go and felt guilty that we didn't, but Ben and Mia usually worked on Sundays and I had a habit of sleeping in on weekends.

Carl put his arms around Mom. "We'll call on Pastor Sonya this evening when the storm has passed."

"I'll try to phone her," Grace said. "That way Pastor Sonya will have all of the ceremony details before Cecelia gets here and we'll all be on the same page. Don't worry, Angela, the wedding will still go off without a hitch."

Mom took a deep breath and nodded, bolstered by Grace's firm grasp on the wedding plans. I wasn't sure how firm her grasp would be if the church ended up flooded and Cecelia didn't show up soon, but for now, Grace was our rock, and I hoped she didn't sink.

THE STORM MOVED out from over town around eight o'clock and the sky lightened to twilight. The sun wouldn't set for about another hour. Monica and I got in her car, and Mom, Carl, and Grace piled into Carl's Mercedes and we all headed across route fifty-two to survey the storm damage to the center of town and look for Cecelia.

She still hadn't answered the calls and text messages, and another call to Judy only confirmed she still hadn't arrived at the Briar Bird. I'd let Ben know to meet us over at the church. Maybe Mom would want him to alert the Brookville Police Department if he was the one to suggest it.

"What are we going to do if the church is flooded?" Monica asked. "Mom will lose it."

"We'll have to talk her into going to the new church."

"Will she still want to go through with the ceremony if Cecelia is missing?"

"I'm not even going to think about that. She has to turn up soon."

We parked beside the church, and Carl pulled up behind us. The ground was wet and muddy, but the water hadn't made it up as far as the church.

"Thank heavens!" Mom exclaimed, rushing up to the side door of the church. "Let's go in and make sure the basement is dry. There's nothing worse than the smell of wet basement."

In my opinion, the church always smelled like mildew, but I kept that thought to myself. Monica and I followed Mom inside with Grace and Carl right behind us.

"This is a beautiful old church," Grace said. "So quaint. I love all of the polished dark wood, and--"

Mom screamed from half way down the aisle.

"Mom!" Monica darted after her, with me right alongside.

Oh good gravy! A woman's feet dangled in mid-air, her heels strewn on the floor beneath her beside an overturned stool.

"Oh dear! Don't look," Carl said behind me. He rushed forward and grabbed Mom, spinning her into him, hiding her eyes against his shoulder and patting her hair.

Grace started forward as if in a trance. She stared at the woman hanging from the choir loft as if she weren't real. "She hung herself."

Ben came through the door followed by our five dogs in bowties. "I brought the ushers to practice," he said.

"Ben," I said, but couldn't get another word out as the dogs swarmed me. They were prancing and smiling with lolling tongues, excited to be in a new place with new scents to sniff.

Gus, my Newfoundland, darted his giant head between my feet and under a pew, knocking me off balance. "Whoa! Gus!" I grabbed the back of Monica and she stumbled into a candelabra, taking it down with us.

Gus barked and tried to burrow under the pew.

"Sit!" Quinn Kelley shouted, darting through the door. The dogs sat and Carl took a knee. Quinn was an official K9 trainer and my sister's fiancé, he had a way of demanding action from dogs, and apparently my mother's groom.

Gus's giant paws skittered backward on the aisle runner, but his head was stuck under the pew. He whimpered and lay down. Quinn reached under and freed the dog's massive head.

"Ben," I said, reaching for the back of a pew to get to my feet. "Look up."

"I see," he said. "Don't go near her, please," he called to Grace who stood underneath the woman. He strode past us toward the front of the church. "I'll take care of this. Cam, can you take everyone else back outside, please? And the dogs?"

"Of course." I hooked my arm through Monica's and hauled her to her feet. We collected Grace and turned her around. "Come with us. Let's go get some air."

Mom and Carl followed Quinn and the dogs out the door with us right behind. "I'm glad Ben stopped by," Carl said. "Poor fella would've been called in anyway."

"It's okay," I said. "He knows his job is 24/7." Not being gone all the time was something he was working on, but getting used to his job being an all hours, night or day, lifestyle career was something I'd had to get used to. It gave us trouble and almost ended our marriage, but ultimately made us more committed than ever to working things out.

"Who was that woman?" Mom asked, wiping her eyes and sniffling, shaken from the awful sight. "I didn't see her face. I couldn't look."

Grace was still in a trance and silent. I'd never seen someone react that way before.

"I guess it wasn't Cecelia," I said, before thinking, "or Grace would've known."

"Heavens no!" Mom scolded. "What would make you say such a thing, Cameron?"

"It was Pastor Sonya," Monica said, her face white as a sheet.

"Pastor Sonya!?" Mom shrieked. "Why would she do that, and today of all days?"

I let the selfish part of her remark slide. I knew it was stress talking.

Ben came outside. "How long were you guys here before me?"

"Maybe two minutes," I said.

"Did you see anyone else?"

I eyed Ben, wondering what he was getting at. "No."

"We didn't either," Carl said. "We pulled up behind Cam and Monica and we all got out and went inside at the same time. That's when we saw her. Angela screamed and you came in."

"Okay, thanks," Ben said. "If you think of anything else you saw that might be relevant, let me know."

"Relevant to what?" I asked. "She hung herself, right?"

"Ben," Quinn said, and nodded to Brutus, Ben's half Rottweiler, half Doberman K9 partner who was sniffing the ground and following a scent around to the side of the church.

Ben nodded and tried to play it off. "Sheriff Reins will be here soon," he said, ignoring my question. "If he wants to ask any other questions I'll call. You all need to leave the scene now."

I tried to pry his thoughts out from his mind through his lips, but the force of my will alone didn't work. Neither did my questioning glare. "I'll see you at home later," he said, and went back inside the church.

"Let's get back to Hilltop Castle and regroup," I said.

Mom threw her hands in the air. "There's no regrouping from

this! We have two pastors in this town. One has no voice and the other's dead. Game over. No wedding."

"Be reasonable, Angela," Carl said. "Reverend Stroup must know other pastors from Brookville or Connorsville churches. He'll be able to find someone else."

"A woman hung herself in the church the day before our wedding, Carl. That's a bad omen. We're not getting married tomorrow."

"Not getting married tomorrow?" Carl shook his head in disbelief. "Of course we are. This is a very unfortunate circumstance, but nothing we can't overcome. We can have the wedding at home if need be."

"No, Carl. I won't have my nuptials plagued by the pastor's suicide. It's too much. It's like a curse."

"A curse?" His eyes grew wide, and I thought we might have a groom gone wild any minute. "That's the most ridiculous thing I've ever heard you say."

"Well, I guess you won't be marrying this ridiculous woman tomorrow, so count your blessings."

"I didn't mean *you* were ridiculous."

"No, just my feelings and emotions."

"Okay, time out," I said. "It's been a long, crazy day and before anyone says anything they don't mean, let's get something to eat, maybe something to drink to take the edge off, and get away from the scene of the crime, so to speak."

"A drink sounds marvelous," Carl said. "Angela, I trust you can get a ride with Cameron and Monica. I'm going to check on things at the restaurant." He turned on his heel and strode to his car.

"Just like a man to leave when the going gets tough," Mom said, watching his Mercedes pull away.

"He's upset," Monica said. "You told him you weren't going to marry him."

"Not tomorrow," she said. "Clearly, not tomorrow."

"I think he might have taken that as you didn't care to get married anyway, so you called it off."

"That's ridiculous." He waved her hand. "He knows I didn't mean never."

"Did he though?" I asked.

Sheriff Reins pulled up and got out of his police cruiser. "Please clear the scene," he said. "The Medical Examiner will be here any moment to collect the body."

"Let me just tell Ben goodbye," I said, and hustled inside the church before Reins could protest.

Ben stood just inside the door. "Is that Reins?" he asked.

"Yes, and I'm leaving, but I want to know one thing before I go."

He put his hands on his hips and narrowed his eyes. "I can't tell you anything, Cam. You know that."

"You asked if we had seen anyone else. Just tell me one thing. Are you treating this as a suicide?"

He sighed, and shook his head. "I'm not ruling out anything yet. There's reason to believe she might not have been alone when this happened. That's all you're getting from me, and here comes the M.E."

"Thanks," I said, and reached up on tiptoe to kiss his cheek. "See you at home later."

I rushed back out the door knowing there was more to Pastor Sonya's death than what our eyes had originally seen. If someone else had been present, it might not have been suicide at all. It might have been murder.

3

Carl had gone off to the Cornerstone, the restaurant and bar he owned, to cool down after Mom announced that she could not get married the next day.

I understood where she was coming from thinking the pastor's death was a bad omen, but I understood Carl's frustration as well. A quiet family ceremony at home would make him happy, and wouldn't interfere with any town mourning or police investigation.

"I wish Cecelia was here," Mom said, taking a sip of red wine. We'd gone back to the castle and were huddled in the great room trying to figure out next steps. "Grace went to check in with Judy at The Briar Bird Inn."

Honestly, it wasn't as if Mom and Cecelia had been close over the years. They kept in touch every six months or so, and sent birthday and Christmas cards. Other than that, I remembered only a handful of times over the decades when they saw one another in person. But, I guess in this circumstance Mom's faith in her friend the wedding planner's ability was unshaken.

"How am I going to get in touch with the florist, the photographer, the bakery..." Mom paced back and forth in the family room at Hilltop

Castle. "I can't even think about the guests coming. What am I supposed to do? Post a notice on the door?"

"I'm sure the whole town has already heard what happened by now," I said. It had been almost two hours and this town was less than two square miles.

"My cell phone is blowing up," Monica said. "So judging by the people who have left voicemails, I think we can spread the word fairly quickly if you're sure you want to postpone."

"Yes, I'm sure," Mom said, waving the thought away. "I can't get married now!"

"Cam and I can start calling people," Monica said. "Do you have your wedding binder with phone numbers for the florist and the other vendors?"

"While you call the vendors, I'll get the Action Agency together and we'll make short work of calling the guests," I said. "We'll just say something vague, like due to an unforeseen event the wedding had to be postponed."

"Say the church flooded," Mom said. "That storm will come in handy as a little white lie."

Everyone would know the truth anyway. An emergency vehicle can't drive two feet down the road in any direction without everyone in town knowing why, but the flood excuse would be more tactful than saying Pastor Sonya was found dead in the church and might have been murdered.

Anyway, the Metamora Action Agency was my team of sleuths. We'd been together for almost a year and had proven our homicide solving abilities time and time again. If it turned out that Pastor Sonya was murdered, we needed to get our ducks in a row and put a suspect list together.

The problem was going to be that the new pastor hadn't been here long. She hadn't known anyone in Metamora for more than a few months--at least not that I knew of. I didn't know anything about her, where she came from, how long she'd been there before coming here... This case would put our abilities to the test.

"Knock, knock," Ben said, opening the front door and coming into the entrance hall. "I found this guy sleeping under a pew. He must have belonged to Pastor Sonya."

In the crook of Ben's arm, he held a pudgy black and white French Bulldog. "Oh, sweetie," Mom ran forward, taking the dog from Ben. "This poor boy. I can't imagine what he's been through today."

"This is Leopold," Monica said, reaching out and reading his name tag. "I didn't know Pastor Sonya had a dog."

"You should keep him, Mom," I said. "I have five at home already." Thankfully, Quinn ushered my fur balls back home after the church disaster.

"And Isobel is enjoying being the only dog at my house," Monica said. Her elderly Shepard lived with my pack for longer than she could stand.

"He must be the reason Gus was trying to burrow under the pew," I said. "Gus must've spotted him under there."

"I guess I can forgive him for that," Monica said, "but I'm going to have a giant bruise on my hip in the morning."

Mom gazed down at Leopold's big dark eyes. "He can stay until we find out if Pastor Sonya had any family who wants to take him."

"I'll run over to Dog Diggity and get some food and supplies," Monica said. She owned a dog boutique that sat among the shops beside the canal. "Cam, come with me."

I wanted to stay and talk to Ben and wheedle more information out of him. "We shouldn't leave Mom," I said.

"We'll be fine, won't we, Leo?" Mom nuzzled her nose into one of Leo's bat-wing-sized ears.

"I'll stay until you get back," Ben said, knowing Mom wasn't quite herself yet.

Especially if she was fostering a dog. She loved mine and even wanted them to be in the wedding as ushers, bowties and all, greeting guests on the church steps, but Mom having her own dog was a big jump.

It wasn't that Mom didn't like animals, she did, but she hated the fur and the mess that came with them. Taking one in so quickly wasn't like her, and I hoped she didn't end up changing her mind after Leo had gotten settled in. The upheaval to his life was already more than the poor guy should have to deal with. I didn't want him doing it twice. Plus I knew if it came to that I'd end up with another dog, and Ben, Mia, and I were already outnumbered almost two to one.

Monica drove back across the busy road and onto the little alley that ran beside the canal. She turned right and drove around the building where Dog Diggity was located and parked behind her shop.

"What do you know?" she asked as we got out of the car.

"What do you mean?"

"Ben told you something. I could tell the second you walked back out of the church right before we left. You had this look, like you were on a mission."

"It's nothing specific."

She unlocked the back door. "Then what vague information did he tell you?"

I stepped inside behind her. "He thinks Pastor Sonya wasn't alone when she died."

Monica stopped and I ran right into her, knocking her into a stack of dog food bags. "Watch where you're going! That's twice today!"

"You stopped! What was I supposed to do? Levitate?" I grabbed her hand and pulled her up off the bags.

"Are you telling me she was murdered?" she asked.

"I don't know. That's all Ben said, that he thinks she wasn't alone."

"Brutus was on the trail of something when we left the church," Monica said. "So we have a potential murdered pastor and a missing wedding planner, all the day before Mom and Carl's wedding. Think they're connected?"

"I can't think anything yet," I said. "Cecelia isn't, technically, a missing person. She's a grown woman whose flight might have been delayed and her phone is probably dead."

"Grace said her flight got in on time at ten this morning."

"Maybe she was mistaken."

"And if she is missing?"

"I don't know, Mon. It would be pretty coincidental."

"I don't believe in that kind of coincidence," Monica said. "I think we need to make sure someone's with Mom all the time."

"I don't think she's in danger," I said.

Monica plucked a canvas shopping tote from behind the counter. "I'm not willing to risk it."

"I'm not willing to risk Mom's life either, and if Cecelia is actually missing, then you might have a point. As of right now, we only have a woman who died by hanging from the choir loft with or without assistance. No murder. No missing person. I'm willing to get the facts before going crazy."

"Now I'm crazy?"

"You're not turning this around on me. You know what I'm saying." Sometimes Monica was a lot like Mom, and this conversation was starting to be a little too déjà vu, reminding me of the one Mom had with Carl earlier. "I'm waiting for facts. We might get more information tonight, and Cecelia could show up any minute. I agree that if she's missing it is a little too coincidental."

"Grab a dog bed from the corner and a couple toys. I'll get food, bones, and a sweater or two."

I picked a blue bed that was soft and plush with a blanket that buttoned onto the back, a duck with a squeaker in the middle, and a teddy bear with a bow tie. "I feel so bad for Leopold. Do you know if she had any other pets?"

"I don't know. It's not a bad idea to find out though so they can be taken care of if so. I should have her address on file since she donates to the animal shelter."

She set the tote of food and chew bones on the floor and rounded the counter to where the register sat. On a shelf underneath, she pulled out a box of index cards. "It's not very modern, but it works. Except, I can't remember her last name." She flipped through the file of cards. "It's not under P for pastor or S for Sonya."

"Is it strange that everyone calls her by her first name, unlike Reverend Stroup?"

"She's a pastor, he's a reverend, does that make a difference?"

"I honestly don't know. I don't think so. I'd think it would be their preference."

Monica kept flipping through her index cards of customer addresses. "Maybe Irene knows her last name."

"Don't make me call Irene. You can't have that many cards in there." I hurried over and tried to grab some index cards to help, but Monica smacked my hand away.

"You'll get them out of order!"

"Fine. You keep looking, and I'll get the Action Agency on the phone."

I called Anna first. She and Logan were my two, newly graduated, high school seniors. They were an item and headed off to college soon. This would probably be their last time working with our team. "Cam?" she said when she answered. "I heard about Pastor Sonya. Is that why you're calling?"

"It is. Kind of. The wedding is on hold for tomorrow. I need help calling all the guests and letting them know."

"Oh. I thought it would be something more interesting. I mean, it's not like I hoped it was another murder, don't get me wrong."

"I know. There might be something there. I have to get more info from Ben. At least we'll all be assembled and ready to dive in if it turns out there's something to investigate."

"I'll call Logan. I'm assuming we'll have to meet at your house since the church is probably blocked off by the police?" The old church basement was our home base. We did all of our work from there.

"For now it is, so yes, we'll meet at my house in an hour."

Next, I called Johnna. She and Roy were my two seniors by age. She originally came my way by order of the court system fulfilling service hours for the town. Johnna had a little kleptomania problem, and Roy was the town drunk. Both of them helped me sell tickets to a town performance when I first started the Metamora Action Agency.

That was before I found a body in the canal and we solved that murder. Unfortunately, we've had to solve a few more since then.

"I'm here with Roy," Johnna said. "He got word about Pastor Sonya from Carl at the Cornerstone and we've been waiting for you to call. When do we meet?"

"My house in one hour."

"Rodger that," she said, and hung up.

Those two were a blessing and a curse. Some days both at the same time.

4

It was nearly ten PM when the Action Agency met at my house, too late to call wedding guests, but not too late for my pack of fur balls to go wild with the company.

"I have bad news," I told the dogs. "Your wedding debut is on hold. Grandma's wedding isn't going to happen tomorrow."

I knew they had no idea that they were even going to be in the wedding tomorrow, let alone be disappointed that it was called off, but I figured I should tell them anyway.

"Sit."

They all plopped down where they stood. "Good boys. Now, go lay down."

They all ran into the family room to wait for me. They knew it was time for their bedtime treats.

Monica had given me some of her newest creations, Blueberry Cheerio Biscuits. She used a dab of honey to combine the crushed cereal and berries and pressed them into star shaped molds. I suspected by the smell that they might have a little peanut butter and banana as well.

Ever since Quinn spent a week getting my boys in line, they'd been the best behaved dogs in town.

"Line up," I told them, something they'd learned just recently. I was able to teach them with Quinn's guidance. Ben's police dog, Brutus would be first in line, but since he was busy working tonight, Gus, my gentle giant, came first. Colby and Jack came next, my twin terrier tanks of mixed blood lines, then our tiny Liam, a Maltese, Yorkie mix. I went down the line and told them to shake, exchanging their paw for a treat and a kiss on the head. They each took their biscuit and found a nice spot to lay down.

"Those hounds are hardly recognizable," Roy said. "They say you can't teach an old dog new tricks, but look at 'em."

"Do you think it's too late to call people?" Anna asked.

"We'll have to start calling in the morning. Tonight we need to figure out everything we can about Pastor Sonya and my mother's wedding planner, Cecelia Evans, who hasn't arrived in town and was due in this morning."

"One murdered, one missing. Got it," Roy said and pointed at Logan. "Take that down."

Logan, already busy taking notes on his laptop just shook his head.

"I'll call the airline," Anna said, "and see if they can tell me if she made the flight."

"Good idea," I said, plopping a plate of cookies down in the middle of the table. We didn't work well without coffee and cookies. At least I didn't work well without them.

"I'll dig up flight information online," Logan said.

"That takes care of them," Johnna said. "Roy and I can work on Pastor Sonya. I've been to that new, uppity church a few times. Had to cost a pretty penny to build it. Stroup went between both churches preaching until that Pastor Sonya arrived. Now he's without a congregation since no services are held at the old place, and it's not just my opinion that he can preach circles around her. That church board over there picked the wrong person."

"Dollars to donuts someone owed her a favor or was bribed into hiring her," Roy said, clucking his tongue and winking. "There's your angle for the murder."

I grabbed a chocolate chip cookie from the plate. "First we need to know if it was murder."

"Having a suspect list puts us ahead of the game, Cameron Cripps Hayman," he said, using my full name like a nickname. I never understood why he did that, but I knew it was a term of endearment now and not a term of suspicion like it once was.

"By all means," I said, "let's get a list together." I crunched on a bite of cookie.

"Could they know each other?" Anna asked. "If we're going to look into both of them, maybe we should search for a connection."

"I don't know how they would," I said. "But I don't know much about either of them, especially Pastor Sonya. Cecelia went to college with my mom at Ohio State. They were in a sorority together and best friends. Cecelia ended up in Los Angeles. I think she lived in Omaha for a while, or maybe Ontario. Somewhere that starts with an O."

"You're a big help," Roy said. "Leave it to me and Johnna. We'll find out about Pastor Sonya and see if their lines crossed anywhere."

"I can't get an answer about an individual passenger from the airlines," Anna said putting her cell phone down on the table.

"Looks like all the flights from Los Angeles that left today before four o'clock PM have arrived in Indianapolis," Logan said, "even if they had connections. Could she have missed her flight and taken a later one that isn't in yet?"

"It's possible," I said. "Anything's possible at this point. Nobody's heard from her."

"Hide nor hair," Roy said. "Was she married? Boyfriend? Someone she wanted to get away from? Maybe she took this opportunity to skip town and start a new life?"

"I think that's the last option we should consider," Anna said.

"And why is that Miss Smarty Pants?" Roy asked. "The police rarely think an adult is missing versus leaving on their own."

"And the police are wrong in most missing persons cases when they think that and waste valuable time. I'm going to search social media for personal connections we can contact for her."

"And get her family all riled up when we don't know anything's wrong?" Johnna asked.

"Maybe they know where she is."

I nodded my agreement. "She might have contacted a family member and let them know where she is."

"And not the bride who's a long time friend?" Johnna said.

"Okay, that's a good point." I had to concede that made sense. "Mom has been in touch with her daily, multiple times a day. Plus, her assistant hasn't heard from her either."

"Who's this assistant and when was the last time she saw her?" Roy asked.

"Her name's Grace. She's in her twenties and works closely with Cecelia and her clients. She saw her yesterday."

"Why didn't they fly here together?" Johnna asked.

"Cecelia told Grace that she and my mom would spend most of the day catching up, so Grace took a later flight since she wouldn't be needed."

"Indeed..." Roy quirked an eyebrow. "Sounds like a suspicious cover story to me."

"Aren't you two working on Pastor Sonya?" Anna asked.

"Am I treading on your toes, Miss College Girl?" Roy asked. "Afraid I'll come to the answer before you?"

"Suspect list, Roy," Johnna said, getting out her knitting. "Get your head back on track."

It seemed that there was something about the rhythmic pattern of knitting that helped Johnna focus. She did all of her best thinking with her needles going at the same time. "We need a congregation list," she said. "The old church passed out a roster so the prayer team had phone numbers."

"We need to know if this newfangled church did something like that," Roy said.

"We can call Irene," I said. "I guess she and Stewart attend there."

"You can call her," Johnna said. "She's your mother-in-law."

"I'm not calling her this late. I'll never hear the end of it."

"Not if you're looking for a prayer team," Anna said. "The pastor of their church is dead and the wedding planner is missing. I think that qualifies for needing prayer."

"Good point," I said. "Let me call her."

I grabbed my handbag, cringing at the thought of digging through all the odds and ends inside to find my phone. I needed to start carrying it in my pocket, or maybe in one of those handy carriers that go around your neck.

I pulled out a pack of allergy pills. The oak trees always killed me in early summer. Next I grasped a calculator. Who knew how long that had been in there since I used the one on my phone. Finally, I found my phone and looked up to four irritated faces around my table.

"We're going through that thing and limiting it to essentials only," Anna said.

"It'll take me two minutes to make a chart showing usage percentages so you know what to get rid of," Logan offered.

"She don't need no chart," Roy said. "I can tell ya now she don't need half the junk in that bag."

Johnna shrugged. "I'm a pack rat, so I can relate."

Pack rat was a nice way of saying kleptomaniac. I wouldn't be tossed in with the same qualifications as Johnna. "Okay! Fine. I'll clean it out."

I dialed Irene and held my breath while it rang. Surprisingly, it only rang once before she answered with a brisk, "Hello, Cameron."

"Hi. Did you hear about Pastor Sonya?"

"Of course I did. I'm in charge of the prayer team. I have a house full right now and we're coordinating our efforts, so if you don't need anything else."

"We'll coordinate with you," I said. "I have my team here as well and we need to contact wedding guests. My mom's decided to postpone the wedding tomorrow. If there's anyone on the list we're both going to call, we might as well pitch in. Two birds, one stone."

"I don't have your mother's wedding invitation list, so how will we do that?"

"If you send us the list of prayer team members you need to call,

Logan can cross reference them on his laptop. It'll only take a minute."

"Hmm, handy. I'll have our secretary email them over to you. It's already late, so if it takes more than ten minutes, we're going to start calling anyway."

"It won't take even ten minutes. I'll get back with you soon."

"Okay, then," she said, and hung up.

I sighed. "The Daughters of Historical Metamora might not be the dictatorship it once was with Irene at the helm, but the new church prayer team has found itself with a new ruler."

"Irene will always find a way to be a bully," Johnna said.

"Nobody stands up to her," Roy said. "Of course she's going to be a bully. It's in her nature. You know who she can't push around? This guy." He pointed his thumbs at himself.

My phone vibrated with an email. "Here's the list of prayer team members." I forwarded the spreadsheet to Logan.

In a couple clicks, he'd compiled the short list of wedding guest that were on Irene's prayer team and emailed it back.

"It's a start," I said, and we had the whole roster plus Pastor Sonya's address.

For the next hour we called Irene's team and woke them up, explaining the awful situation with their pastor passing away, the postponed wedding plans, the missing wedding planner, and asking for their prayers.

Listening to my Action Agency take on this difficult task with empathy and tact, I couldn't help being proud of how far we'd come in the past year. This rag tag, mismatched team had become a cohesive unit that knew how to work as professionals.

That was until Roy shouted, "You were there, weren't ya? You killed her," and started laughing like a hyena.

He put his hand over his phone when he noticed us all staring. "It's Stewart. He already knows everything. He's makin' fun of us poking our noses into a suicide."

"It's not a laughing matter," I said, crumbling my cookie in my hand. I could feel the anger taking over. "If you can't take this seriously then you have no business helping us."

"I'm sorry," he said, ducking his head. "You're right. It's just Stewart was joking around and I got carried away."

"I know you didn't know Pastor Sonya. That doesn't mean we take her death lightly."

"You're right. I was out of line." He put the phone to his ear and said, "Stew, I gotta run," and hung up. "Won't happen again," he told us, looking around the table.

Just then it hit me. "You haven't taken any drinks from your flask."

Roy patted his chest where his inside pockets were located in his sports coat, where he always stored his flask. "No ma'am, I'm giving it up."

"Drinking? You're giving up drinking?" I was shocked.

"Only coffee and tea for me," he said.

Johnna nodded her head. "It's true. I've been keeping a close eye on him."

"That's amazing, Roy," Anna said. She reached over and patted his hand.

"It really is," Logan agreed.

"I don't know what to say," I said. "I'm so impressed. What made you decide to stop drinking?"

He glanced over at Johnna. "It was time," he said.

"Well, I'm proud of you, Roy," I said. "If I can help you stay on the wagon, please let me know."

"Will do," he said, beaming. "It's been five days, and so far it's been hard but not the worst thing I've ever been through."

As a Vietnam vet, I knew it wasn't even close to anything he went through over there. One thing Roy Lancaster always managed to do was surprise me.

5

The wedding day arrived with bright blue skies, birds singing, and my dad knocking on my door. I swung it open wearing my bathrobe, old socks with holes in them--I couldn't find my slippers since the dogs used them for hide and seek--and my hair standing up all over my head. "Dad? I didn't know you were coming."

Seeing as how he'd been traveling the world and called me at random times of day to tell me where he was and what he was up to--the pyramids in Giza, ice caves in Juneau, Victoria Falls in Africa--it was a shock to find him on my front porch at seven in the morning.

"Monica didn't tell you I was coming?" He stepped past me into the house with a suitcase.

"No. It must've slipped her mind." And I'd give her a piece of my mind as soon as I saw her.

"I came for the wedding."

"Oh. Mom didn't tell me she--"

"Your mother doesn't know."

"Dad, you're not going to try to stop the wedding are you? It's already stopped, but if it were going to happen today, was that your plan?"

He dropped his suitcase beside the kitchen table. "What do you mean it's already stopped?"

Before I could answer, he had me in a bear hug. Dad's a big man, tall and broad, and I felt my back crack. He smelled of Old Spice and had perpetual stubble on his cheeks. When he let go, I motioned for him to sit down at the table. "I'll get coffee going."

Ben came down the stairs and saw my dad. "Joe, is that you? I didn't know you were coming to town."

"Surprise," Dad said. "Monica forgot to tell Cameron." He stood up and he and Ben shook hands and did that around the back pat thing that men did instead of hugging.

"Are you here for the wedding?"

"I was, but Cameron said it's been called off. Angela lost her mind before our wedding day, but I figured she'd be calmer this time."

"She lost her mind, that's for sure," I said, sitting a cup of coffee in front of him, "but that's not why it's postponed."

Ben took the cup I held out for him. "There was an unfortunate incident at the church last night."

"What? Did it flood? They can have it at their house. From what I understand it's enormous."

"It's a literal castle," I said. "But, she doesn't want to do that."

"Don't tell me Angela is being irrational," Dad said, giving a little chuckle. "That woman is the most stubborn person I've ever met."

"They don't have anyone to marry them," I said. "The pastor's dead. She hung herself in the church last night."

Dad sputtered, spitting coffee down the front of his shirt. "What? A pastor? Aren't they supposed to be against suicide?"

"I doubt she was a proponent," Ben said, catching the kitchen towel I tossed to him for Dad.

I poured myself a cup of coffee and sat on the other side of Dad across from Ben at our round table. "We don't know what happened," I said. "The wedding planner never showed up either."

"Cecelia? What do you mean she never showed up? I saw her a few weeks ago when I was out in LA."

"You were in LA?"

"Did she say anything about her plans for coming here?" Ben asked.

"Of course," Dad said, wiping his shirt. "Well, not specific plans. She said she'd be getting in the day before and hoped Angela would relax and spend some time catching up before diving into wedding details. She said something about getting their nails done or going to a spa nearby. I don't know, I stopped listening when she started talking about beauty regimens."

I made a mental note to check out spas nearby, or any between Metamora and Indianapolis.

"I'm sure she'll show up today," Dad said. "I've known Cecelia since college and one thing that's never changed is her ability to be late everywhere she goes."

"Nothing else she said stood out to you?" I asked.

"No. She seemed stressed. Tired. There was some kerfuffle with a recent wedding that had her questioning if she was ready to retire."

"Retire? Really? I wonder if Mom knows what that's about?"

"Probably not if there was something that didn't go right," Ben said. "I doubt a wedding planner would tout her failures to one of her clients, no matter how long she's been friends with her."

"Right," Dad said. "Especially since Cecelia knows your mother and how she overreacts."

"Her assistant mentioned how she hasn't been in the best health and was stressed. She called her fragile."

Ben took a sip of coffee, the lines in his forehead creasing as he considered this new information. "Maybe she took off," he said. "If she was pushed too far and had enough, she might have just gone off somewhere."

"Nervous breakdown?" Dad asked.

"Possibly. It's not unheard of."

I shook my head. "There is no way she'd do that to Mom. They've been talking multiple times a day. If there was any indication that something was wrong, Mom would know."

"Not if something happened yesterday morning and Cecelia went into a tailspin and took off," Dad said. "I doubt she would've planned it out, but if her bag was packed and she could get away, she might have just gone."

"I need to talk to Grace," I said, pushing my chair back from the table. "She's the only one who knows the details of what's happening in Cecelia's life."

"Better check on Angela and see how she's doing with the dog," Ben said.

"Angela with a dog?" Dad laughed. "She's always liked them, but never wanted one of her own. Too much fur and poop to clean up."

"That's what I'm afraid of," I said. "I don't want the pastor's poor dog to be shuffled around too much after losing his owner."

"If he travels well, I'll take him," Dad said. "Always wanted a dog and your mother wouldn't let me have one."

"Monica was allergic," I said.

"She's taking allergy pills now and she's got her own dog," he said. "Don't think the doctor didn't say we could get one. Your Mom didn't want the bother of a pet."

"I'll get dressed and go check on them."

Then I'd track down Grace and stop by Pastor Sonya's house to make sure there weren't other animals in need of care.

"Guess I'm coming with you," Dad said. "At least until Little Mia wakes up and can spend some time with Grandpa Joe."

"Did you tell her about the wedding?" I asked Ben.

He shook his head. "She was sleeping when I got home last night. I take it you didn't?"

"*I* was sleeping when *she* got home last night." Having a teenager who had a midnight curfew on weekends was rough. I tried to stay awake until she got home, but often failed. "I know she stuck her head in and told me she was home. I glanced at the clock to make sure she wasn't late, but that's all I remember."

"She can wear the bridesmaid dress to Homecoming," Ben said. "I'm sure that's what she'll be the most upset about."

His cell phone rang and he picked it up from the kitchen counter where it was plugged in charging. "It's Mia," he said, glancing at the display, "calling from upstairs. Good morning, Sunshine," he said, answering. "Did we wake you? Grandpa Joe's here." He listened, then smirked. "I know...okay, I'll tell them."

He hung up and chuckled. "I forget how grown up she is. She wanted me to tell you that she'll be down in a minute and not to leave before she says hi. She has to work today at the Soda Pop Shop, but wants Joe to come in to see her, and she says she's not wearing that dress to Homecoming, it's too plain."

"The walls have ears," I said.

Dad let out a boisterous laugh. "I'll treat everyone to breakfast when you're ready to go," he called to Mia through the ceiling, knowing she was listening.

"I have to get back to work," Ben said. "I'll take a raincheck."

"Then maybe tonight we can grill out and I'll cook up some of my famous steaks."

"I'll take you up on that. I haven't had one of those in years." Ben got up from the table and chugged down the rest of his coffee. "Try to keep your daughter out of trouble today," he teased.

"Out of your business you mean," I said.

"Exactly."

"I'll do my best. My ladies are head strong," Dad said.

"You can say that again." Ben gave me a wink.

The problem was I needed a way into his business. Brutus had sniffed out a clue yesterday. It was a shame dogs couldn't talk or I'd only have to give him a biscuit to tell me what he'd found. Too bad Ben wasn't as easy to bribe with treats.

WE GAVE Monica a call and told her to meet us at the Soapy Savant for breakfast, then me, Dad, and Mia headed over to get a table. We ordered coffee and I excused myself to step outside and call Mom.

"Did I wake you?" I asked her when she answered.

"No, I didn't get much sleep last night."

"How are you doing this morning? Any word from Cecelia?"

"Not a word. I'm worried, Cameron. And Carl is so upset with me.

I don't know how he doesn't realize this is a terrible start to a marriage. Going through with the wedding today would be asking for trouble."

"Did you talk to him about setting a new date?"

"No, he won't talk about it."

"I'm sorry, Mom. He'll come around. It was a blow to him for you to cancel. How's Leopold?"

"He's a wonderful dog, quiet and mannered. He hasn't had any accidents and slept beside me in bed all night."

"That's good to hear. I'm going to try to find out where Pastor Sonya lived to make sure there aren't any other pets at her house. Call if you need anything. We'll probably stop by later."

We said goodbye and hung up. As I was jamming my phone in my back pocket, Monica came up the sidewalk.

"Hey, Cam! I forgot to tell you, Dad's coming to town." She laughed. "That's what I tried to tell you in Mom and Carl's basement tavern, and then I forgot."

"At least you tried." I held the door to the Soapy Savant open for her. "We got a table already."

Halfway to the table, Monica stopped dead in her tracks. I stepped on the back of her shoe, but luckily was able to hop to the side and keep from running into her this time. "Would you stop doing that?"

"Why is Carl sitting with Dad and Mia?"

I looked around her and was just as confused. "Oh, good gravy. I have no idea. He wasn't there when I went outside to call Mom."

We hurried over to make sure things stayed civil, but immediately realized there was no need to worry. "She'll come around, Carl," Dad was saying. "It's got nothing to do with you. It's like those superstitions around wedding days. Wearing something blue in the rain or whatever they say."

"I suppose you're right," Carl said. "It's still a disappointment."

"At our age, I can see why you're rushed, but it's not like you're waiting to get married for all the good stuff." He clucked his tongue and shrugged his brows at Carl.

"Dad!" Monica said, and side-eyed Mia.

Mia laughed. "Please, I'm going to be a senior. I know what he's talking about. I'm not a baby."

"No, it's not that," Carl said. "I'm just an old man who wants a wife to settle down with. It's been a long time and that castle's a big place to live alone in."

"She hasn't moved out," I said. "She's home worried about how upset you are. She wants to talk about setting a new date."

"I'll go talk to her. I feel terrible about how selfish I've reacted."

"You're not selfish," I said. "There's no one way to react to something like this. The two of you just need to keep moving forward. It didn't impact your relationship, only your wedding plans."

"And those can be re-scheduled," Monica said. "Well, sort of. I didn't get in touch with the florist yet. They open in an hour. The caterer did answer last night, but said it was too late to cancel, and they already had most of the dishes prepped. It was the same with the cake."

"Sounds like you're having a party," Dad said to Carl.

"Heaven help me, Angela will have a goose if they bring flowers and food to the house. I better get back home."

"We'll be over right after we eat," I said. "I need to track down Grace and ask her a few questions. Hopefully, we'll find Cecelia today and Mom will have one less thing on her mind to worry about."

Carl left and Soapy, the mayor and owner of the cafe, came over to take our order. "Poor Carl and Angela," he said. "I was hoping to get a break to come chat before he left."

"You heard, huh?" I asked.

"Everybody's heard. It's all anyone has been talking about this morning."

"What are they saying?"

"Well, nobody can believe it of course. Pastor Sonya had planned a summer Bible camp for the younger kids that's scheduled to kick off next week. She hadn't been talking like someone who wouldn't be around. She has weddings booked for just about every Saturday this summer."

"Oh, my."

"I don't think it sounds like something that was in character for her," Soapy said. "Not one person has said she was depressed. From what I gather, she was very happy to be here at the new church and talking about fundraising for a new pre-school she wanted to open at the church in a couple years."

"Usually people who are thinking about taking their own lives aren't planning for the future at the same time," Monica said. "That does sound strange."

We each ordered a breakfast sandwich and Soapy left the table to get coffee refills. "We need to get over to Pastor Sonya's house," I said. "None of this is sitting right with me. There's got to be more to this than meets the eye."

"There always is," Monica said.

Between Pastor Sonya's death and Cecelia's disappearance, I wasn't sure which was more bizarre. One thing I knew for certain was that things that seemed to have no rhyme or reason always did in the end. I just had to find the pieces of this puzzle and fit them together.

6

Pastor Sonya lived on the edge of Metamora just outside Connorsville in a little brick ranch that had been added onto in the back. The yard was small and surrounded by a white picket fence. Well-tended flower beds in bloom hugged the foundation of the house. It was story book. It looked like a pastor's home, somewhere where nothing bad could ever happen.

"How do we get inside?" Monica asked.

"I don't know. I didn't think that far ahead." I bent down and moved the welcome mat. "No key under here. Let's keep looking for a spare."

"I'll check around back," she said, and descended the porch stairs to take the sidewalk around.

I checked all the planters, the bird feeder, rocks that I thought could be one of those fake key hiders, and turned up nothing. I ran my hand along the top of the doorframe, and behind the bushes along the window sills. I checked all of the obvious places people hide spare keys and didn't find one.

Then the front door opened and Monica smiled at me. "Come on in. The back door was unlocked."

"Good, I was just about to weigh our odds of going to jail for breaking and entering."

"We could always say we heard another dog, or a cat, or a bird...thought we saw a goldfish bowl."

"Ben might buy dog or cat, but goldfish would be pushing it."

The inside of the house was tidy and cool with the AC running. There was a small cross on the wall beside a painting of a lion and a lamb. A Bible sat on the coffee table next to a vase of silk flowers. The room gave off a church office vibe and I had the impression this is where she'd entertain parishioners.

"Kind of stuffy looking in here," Monica said.

"I think it's the chintz floral sofa that's doing it," I said. "Let's check out the kitchen."

We stepped into a bright, lemony yellow room with white frilly curtains and a vintage, 1970's Formica table with matching plastic covered chairs.

"I love this," Monica said, running her hand over the laminate table. "Mom and Dad used to have one in the basement, remember?"

"Yeah, we used to play Barbies under it."

"And Mom and Dad would have card parties down there." She frowned. "They always seemed happy together."

"They were back then, Mon. It just didn't last."

"What if Quinn and I get married and it doesn't last?"

"Do you think it will? Does it feel like it will?"

"I said yes to his proposal, so of course I feel like it'll last."

"There you go. You can't see into the future, so use your best judgement based on what you have to go by today."

"You're so romantic, Cameron," she said, scowling at me and walking off down the hallway toward the bedrooms.

"What? I'm being honest. I could say you're going to live forever in a mansion with five kids, three dogs, two cars, a vacation home in Tahiti--"

"I don't want a vacation home in Tahiti!"

"Monica, you just have to love him, be best friends with him, have fun together, laugh a lot, and take things one day at a time. I'm no expert, but that's what I'm trying to do."

"I can do that," she said, and reached back to take my hand. "Thanks."

"That's what I'm here for."

There were four doors off the hallway. One was a small bathroom. I flipped on the light. The rug, toilet seat cozy and towels were all pink and the shower curtain was ivory lace. "Not much to see in here." I gave the medicine cabinet a quick once over, but nothing out of the ordinary stood out.

The three bedroom doors were closed. "I'll take this one," I said, pointing to the farthest one on the left.

"Guess I'll be across the hall."

I turned the knob and opened the door. The air was stagnant, and it was dark like the room had black out curtains. I ran my hand along the wall to find a light switch, but couldn't find one.

I eased my way into the room, reaching in front of me through the darkness trying not to run into anything. Paper crushed under my feet, and something that felt like a sweater wrapped around my shoe. "This place is a mess," I said. It's always the neat freaks in public who were litter bugs in their own homes.

"It's a mess in here too. Looks like it's been ransacked."

I tried to kick my foot free of the sweater and took another step forward. The toe of my left sneaker caught on something and I stumbled forward, whacking my knee into a dresser. "Son of a bee sting!"

I bent forward and grabbed my throbbing knee, only to hit my forehead on the same dresser, lose my balance and crash down onto the floor.

"Cameron? Are you okay?"

I lay there for a minute with my head spinning, catching my breath and taking inventory of all my parts. "Well, nothing's broken. I guess that counts as okay."

I reached out to get up on all fours, and grasped one of someone else's fours--specifically, a foot.

I shot to my feet like I'd been fired from a cannon, holding my hand like it was scorched. "Monica get in here I just touched a foot!"

"A foot?" She sounded skeptical at best, but came across the hall and stood in the doorway. "Why didn't you turn on the light?"

"There is no light!"

She turned her cell phone flashlight on and shined it up to the ceiling. "It's a ceiling fan. You just have to pull the--"

"Monica, there is a body on this floor!"

She shined her light down to where I was standing. "Holy crow! Isn't that Cecelia?"

"I grabbed Cecelia's foot? Why is Cecelia laying on the floor in Pastor Sonya's bedroom without her shoes on?"

"Cam, calm down. Is she alive?"

"I don't know! Her foot was cold!"

Monica nudged me aside and knelt to feel for a pulse. "Call 911. She's gone."

"Why do I have to find all the dead bodies in town? Isn't it someone else's turn?"

"I'll call 911. You go outside and try to just breathe and calm down."

"It's one thing to find them, but now I have to fall on top of one? Is this my destiny? Will I be the town's murder magnet forever?"

"Let's hope there isn't another one. We've had enough to last us for at least fifty years."

I don't remember how I got there, but I was sitting on the front porch step when Sheriff Reins pulled up. "Can there be one police call in this town where I show up and don't find you?" he asked me.

"That's what I'm saying! I don't want to always be here either."

"Then why are you? Stop sticking your nose in where it doesn't belong."

His words pulled me back to myself faster than a cold bucket of water would have. If it weren't for me and my team sticking our noses in, I have no doubt most of the murders that had happened in this town wouldn't have been solved. My husband was a good officer, but he didn't have an insider who heard all the low down from the

Daughters of Metamora, like Johnna. He didn't have Roy, who was a confidant to all the older gentlemen in town. He didn't have a super computer geek like Logan, or a teen genius like Anna. Our combined abilities made all the difference in the cases we solved, and *that* was why I always stuck my nose in, and I guess it was also why I was always the one finding the bodies.

I just wished they'd stop showing up to begin with.

"I KNEW THEY WERE CONNECTED SOMEHOW," Monica said, placing the plate of cookies on the table. "I just had a feeling."

"I did too," Anna said.

The Action Agency had gathered at my house again. Monica made me sit and drink iced tea and not move until she deemed me to be back in my right mind. I told her I was fine now, but she refused to believe me. Sometimes, I think she just liked being in charge.

"The bedrooms had both been searched," she said. "We didn't get to look in the third one, but the one I'd been in had a little desk that had the drawers pulled out and all of the contents dumped onto he floor."

"I was stepping on papers I think," I said. "And there were clothes on the floor that I kept getting my feet stuck in. Maybe they dumped the dresser drawers?"

"Sounds like Cecelia was doing some searchin' and got herself caught," Roy said.

"That's a logical conclusion considering she was found without shoes in a bedroom," Logan said. "Shoes would leave tracks in the carpet."

"Or track blood," Anna added. "Maybe she went there to find Pastor Sonya and murder her."

"What a morbid thought," Johnna said.

"She could be on to something," I said. "But if that was the case and Cecelia didn't find her, then who found Cecelia? And who killed

Pastor Sonya if there was another person at the scene of what appeared to be her suicide?"

"Two dead women, both around the same age." Roy scratched his head. "I sure could use a drink, but I'll settle for a cup of coffee."

"I've got a pot," Monica said. "Let me get you a cup."

"I appreciate it," he said.

"We need the time of their deaths," Logan said. "The one who died last could have murdered the first."

"I don't know how we'll get that," I said, "but I'll try to get it out of Ben."

"What would someone be searching for in a pastor's house?" Monica asked.

"We need to find out. If Cecelia was the one searching and she didn't make it out of the house, there's a chance that what she was looking for is still there." I had a spark of an idea forming. "What if we offered to do something at the house? Plan something, like a vigil?"

"Then we could sneak inside," Anna said, catching on.

"Isn't that sacrilegious?" Johnna asked, looking up from her knitting. "Manipulating a vigil for a murdered pastor?"

"All of a sudden you're Dorothy Do Gooder," Roy said. "Even if it ain't a very pious thing to do, solving a murder is the greater good here. I don't think old Saint Pete will hold it against ya at the gates."

"Drink your coffee you old sourpuss," Johnna shot back at him, resuming her knitting. "Saint Pete's already got my name flagged."

"Guess we best get you some brownie points then," he said.

"Okay, here's the plan," I said. "We have the list of the prayer team members at the new church. We'll call and spread the word about a vigil at Pastor Sonya's house, but don't give anyone your name or Irene will be on us for stepping on her toes since she's in charge of them. If someone asks, we're parishioners spreading the word about the vigil."

"Lying and manipulating," Johnna said, and sighed.

"I can't make any of you participate. I'd never do that. This is all voluntary. If you aren't comfortable with the plan, please, don't do it. I don't want you feeling guilty about any of this."

Johnna grumbled to herself and kept knitting. I wasn't sure what was happening with her. She wasn't normally conflicted or moody.

"Mom got the candles delivered with the flowers," Monica said. "She should have about three dozen ivory tapers that were going to be at the end of each pew and in candelabras at the ceremony and reception. I'm sure we can use them for the vigil instead."

"That's perfect. Who can lead the vigil? Reverend Stroup lost his voice."

"What are we planning?" Dad asked, strolling in the kitchen from the living room where he'd been napping on the couch.

"A vigil for the pastor," Monica said. "But we're not sure who we can get to lead the prayers."

"I'm an ordained minister. Even if it was by a dodgy monk I met outside of Nepal who charged me twenty bucks, I got a certificate."

"Ordained in Buddhism?" I asked.

"I'm not clear on that exactly. The whole thing was kind of sketchy and I had a head cold and was taking a lot of medicine."

"It was probably a fever dream," Roy said.

"I thought that, too," Dad said, chuckling, "but then there was the certificate in my hotel room to prove it happened."

I glanced around the table. Anna shrugged. Logan was busy typing into his laptop, probably looking up ordination by sketchy monks in Nepal. Johnna wouldn't look up from her knitting. Roy nodded his approval of the plan, and Monica said, "Why not? What have we got to lose? He can say prayers like anyone else and he does have a certificate."

"Irene's going to lose her mind," I said.

Dad laughed. "Sounds like the best reason to do it, then."

"We'll start calling people on the list," Anna said.

"Thanks," I said, and looked over at Monica. "Let's go get the candles, and break the bad news about Cecelia to Mom. I really don't want to be the one to tell her."

“What’s the bad news?” Dad asked.

“She’s dead,” Roy said. “Sherlock and Watson over here found her in the pastor’s house while they were snoopin’.”

“That’s a shame,” Dad said. “She was a good one.”

The town knew something was going on at Pastor Sonya's house, but since she lived alone and the police weren't releasing any names or information yet, nobody knew what was happening. The only people who knew Cecelia was dead were sitting in my kitchen.

"I'm not telling her!" Monica folded her arms in a firm stance against her involvement.

"I'll tell her," Dad said. "We were married for a long time. I'm a pro at upsetting her. The trick is to make her think it's worse than what it is, so when you come out with the bad news, it's not as terrible as she thought."

"What's worse than her good friend and wedding planner being killed?" Anna asked.

Dad got a shrewd look on his face. "Just let me handle it."

I knew it was a bad idea. I felt it in every ounce of my being, but I really didn't want to be the one to tell her. "Fine. You can tell her."

Dad grabbed his wallet and his phone from the kitchen counter. "I'm going to need to make a stop on the way."

7

Dad wanted to stop at a funeral home. He ran inside and came back out with a brochure listing burial costs along with services provided and casket models.

"What on earth will Mom need that for?" I asked, backing out of the funeral home parking lot. "She's not going to be the one responsible for the funeral."

"Trust me," Dad said. "I know your mother."

"You're divorced from my mother. I'm not sure you're the one I should be listening to."

"Do you want to tell her? I'm happy to step aside."

"No. We'll go with your plan."

"That's what I thought. I just need to tell Carl his part in this. Do you know his number?"

I rattled off Carl's cell phone number, and Dad dialed.

"Monica," I said, "talk to me so I don't hear anything he's saying and can't be held accountable for it."

"You know what I don't get?" she said. "How would someone be able to enter the church in that storm and not leave any trace? No mud or wet footprints. At least none that we saw offhand. Not that we were looking for anything like that."

"The floor is linoleum though, so it would've been wet and slick."

"Do you think whoever was in there with Pastor Sonya had been inside since before the storm started?"

It was a definite possibility. "I guess we need to consider that. I know there's a quilting circle who use the old sacristy to set up their frame. They meet on Tuesday and Thursday mornings."

"We'll talk with them. Any other groups or people who are regularly in there?"

"Other than the Action Agency? Sometimes Reverend Stroup's church secretary, Opal Mavis, but she's only there when he is and then just part time."

"We need to talk to her, too, and Reverend Stroup."

"You've got quite the hit list," Dad said.

"It's not a hit list, it's a suspect list," Monica said.

"You're going to hit them up with questions, aren't you?"

"I suppose we are."

"Then they're a hit list."

I wasn't going to get involved in that debate. He could call it what he wanted, but the fact was we had a lot of people to talk to and not a lot of clues.

Carl was on his way out when we arrived at Hilltop Castle. "Don't forget," Dad told him.

Carl looked harried and frazzled and nodded his agreement as he dashed out the door.

"Good man," Dad said, watching him go.

"I'm not sure he should be taking advise from you, either," I said.

"Nobody wants to be the bad guy. I volunteered." He held up the funeral brochure and smacked it against his palm. "Now, where's your mother?"

"Mom?" Monica called while we kicked our shoes off near the suit of armor.

"This place is a riot," Dad said, looking around and smiling. "Like Carl's got a King Arthur complex."

"It's about time you got here," Mom called from the direction of the living room. "I'm drowning in flowers and cake. The caterer is going to be here with enough food for a hundred people any minute."

She came around the corner and stopped stiff when she spotted Dad. "Hello, Joseph. What are you doing in town?"

"Honestly, Ange, I came for your wedding."

"You weren't invited."

"You needed someone to give you away. I figured your father gave you away to me, so it was on me to give you to someone else."

Mom pursed her lips. "I'm not sure if I should be angry about that, so I'm going to let it go for now."

His gesture had struck me right in the heart, and in a very straight forward way, it made sense.

"Well, I'm afraid I have some bad news." He bowed his head. "Grandma Nina has passed." He held out the brochure for her to take. "You knew her best."

"Oh no!" Mom put her hands to her face. Tears filled her eyes.

"Dad?" I said, not on board with this farce.

"Are you very upset?" Dad asked her.

"Of course I'm upset! I haven't seen her since before our divorce, but your grandmother was a very special person to me."

"Okay, so what if I told you someone had died, but it wasn't Granda Nina?"

"Joseph? What are you getting at?" The wrath in Mom's voice was building by the syllable.

"It's Cecelia who's dead. Does that make it any better?"

"Joseph! Is this another lie, or is it real? Is Cecelia really dead?"

"Yes, Mom," I said. "Monica and I found her this morning. I'm sorry."

"Oh." Mom put her hand to her chest and stepped back, her misty eyes overflowing. "I had a feeling. How did it happen?"

"Looks like she was murdered in the dead pastor's house," Dad said.

"What? Why was she in Pastor Sonya's house? Who killed her?"

"We don't know yet," Monica said. "We don't know the cause of death either. Ben and the police are still at the house processing things."

"Does Carl have room to freeze or refrigerate the catering at the Cornerstone?" I asked. "It might be better to have the food dropped off there if he does."

Mom nodded. "I was going to still have everyone over for an engagement party since we couldn't cancel the food and cake and flowers, but now I can't see how I'll be up for that."

"I'll send Carl a text and call the caterer," Monica said.

Mom nodded, absentmindedly. "Okay."

"Let me get you some hot tea, Mom," I said. "Go sit down."

"Put a little Irish whiskey in that tea," Dad said, taking Mom by the arm. "It's good for a shock like this. Come with me, Ange, let's get you on the couch."

Monica and I hustled, her making calls and me making hot tea. We needed to tell Grace what happened to Cecelia as well. I didn't think Mom looked up for that conversation, so Monica and I would have to do it if Ben hadn't already found her. If anyone knew who to contact in Cecelia's family, it would be Grace.

The faint click of dog nails sounded on the tile kitchen floor. I turned to find Leopold standing next to me looking up with a tilted head and wide eyes. "This is all confusing for you, isn't it?" I bent and picked him up. He weighted about twenty-five pounds and was shaped like a little pig. He had an underbite that made his two bottom canine teeth stick out over his top lip. I kissed the top of his head and he smelled like perfume. It was familiar, but not Mom's, so it had to be Pastor Sonya's. It was a sweet scent, like cotton candy. Not something I'd pick for a pastor in her sixties or even for myself, but she must've liked it. I'd have to ask Ben if he could get the perfume bottle from the pastor's house and we could spray some on one of Leopold's stuffed toys to comfort him.

I found his treats and gave him one before taking the hot tea to Mom. He followed me into the living room and hopped up on the sofa next to her. She reached down and stroked his fur, and I could tell it comforted them both.

"Come over to Cam's tonight with Carl," Dad said. "I'm grilling steaks. Surround yourself with family and you'll feel better."

Mom sniffled and nodded.

"Mom," I said, "we're planning a vigil for later tonight. Since they delivered the candles, can we use them?"

"Sure," she said, wiping her eyes. "I need to get Grace on the phone."

"Give us her number," Monica said. "We'll tell her."

"Are you sure?"

"We're sure."

"Her number's in my phone on the table over there." She pointed across the room and Monica fetched her phone. "I can't imagine how she'll take this news. Just have her come over here. We'll all tell her together."

Monica handed me the phone. "Thanks," I said, giving her a not so nice look. I started to look for Grace's contact number, and thought twice about it. "This is really something we should tell her in person. Let's go by the Briar Bird and see if she's there. I'm surprised she isn't here helping with the wedding postponement."

"So am I," Mom said. "I tried her earlier and didn't get an answer.

"I'll stay here with your mother until Carl gets back," Dad said.

"Mom?" I asked, waiting for her to shove Dad off the couch and tell him to go with us. Instead she just waved me off. "Go ahead."

I certainly didn't peg Carl for a jealous man, but I didn't know what he'd think about coming home to find Dad there alone with Mom on what was supposed to be his wedding day.

"Let's hurry," I told Monica as we buckled in and headed down the steep driveway past the gatehouse. "The last thing we need is Dad upsetting her more."

"No, Cam, the last thing we need is to find another body. Where do you think Grace has been all day?"

"You don't think..."

Monica shrugged. "Someone with connections to Pastor Sonya and Cecelia isn't in town for the wedding. I just hope Grace hasn't crossed paths with that person."

With that thought, I pressed down harder on the accelerator. We needed to find Grace before any harm came to her.

8

Judy Platt stood at the hostess stand in the lobby of the Briar Bird Inn that served as a place to check in and get a table for her restaurant. "Sorry, I haven't seen Grace since she checked in yesterday evening. Poor girl was shaken to the core after finding Pastor Sonya."

"She was in a kind of stupor," Monica said.

"Can we see if she's in her room?" I asked. "Mom hasn't been able to reach her today and we have some important news to share with her."

Judy glanced left then right, making sure nobody was listening. "Does it have to do with the stranger they found in Pastor Sonya's house?"

Monica and I looked at each other before nodding, yes. Might as well admit it, the news was already spreading.

"She's in the Bird's Eye View room on the top floor. Go on up."

We headed up the stairs. The first floor had five bedrooms with names like Night Owl, Snow Bird, and Crow's Feet. A narrow spiral staircase took us to the third floor where there were two more large rooms. Bird's Eye View was in the front of the house and looked out over the downtown area with the shops and the canal.

I knocked on the door. "Grace? It's Cameron and Monica." I waited a few seconds and knocked again. "Grace?"

There was some shuffling behind the door and it opened. Grace stood there with her hair messed, mascara running down her cheeks from the day before, and generally looking like she'd been hit by a bus.

Monica stepped in the room and took Grace's hands. "Are you okay? You don't look it. Have you had anything to eat or drink today?"

"That was the first time I've ever seen her--a dead person," Grace said. "I can't believe she was hanging there like that."

"I know," Monica said, walking Grace toward the bathroom, "it was awful. Let me help you get that makeup off. Do you mind if Cameron gets you a change of clothes from your suitcase?"

"No, I don't mind." Her eyes began to tear. "Thank you. I didn't know what to do. I should be helping Angela. I just couldn't face getting out of bed."

While Monica helped Grace wash her face, brush her teeth, and comb her hair, I opened her suitcase. I found a pair of khaki capri pants and a pink, eyelet short sleeved blouse. I wasn't anxious to rifle around in her underwear, but thankfully there were modest white cotton ones like I bought for Mia, reminding me she was a young girl, most likely just out of college and trying to find her place in the world. I really hoped finding Pastor Sonya didn't do any permanent damage to her confidence.

I grabbed a makeup bag, a little jar of moisturizer, and a bottle of perfume to hand over to Monica with Grace's clothes. "Is there anything else you need?" I asked.

"This is everything," Grace said, giving me a shy smile. "Thanks."

The room had a small sitting area beside the window where Monica and I sat while we waited for Grace to change clothes and finish getting ready.

"She's not going to take this well," Monica whispered.

"We need to find out if we should send for one of her parents or a sibling to fly home with her. She's not stable now and she didn't even know Pastor Sonya."

My phone vibrated with a text message. "It's Anna," I said. "They've called everyone and are expecting around fifty people for the vigil. They told everyone eight PM."

"Are we going to be allowed on the property?"

"I don't know. I'll have to check with Ben to find out."

"Should we tell Grace about Cecelia here or back at Mom's?"

"At Mom's," I whispered. "We didn't even really know Cecelia. I think it would help if Mom was there when we told her."

The bathroom door opened and Grace came out. With her hair pulled back in a ponytail, no makeup, and casual clothes on she looked all of sixteen.

I didn't know how we would tell her about Cecelia without totally crushing her.

9

Carl opened the door when we got back to Hilltop Cassel with Grace. He seemed even more distressed than he had when we saw him leaving the house earlier. "Do you know who Jimmy Chews is?" he asked us, wringing his hands. "Your father told me to find Jimmy Chews to cheer up your Mom, but I've asked all over town and nobody knows who he is."

"Do you mean Jimmy Choo's, the shoes?" Monica asked. "That's a brand name. He's a designer famous for his pumps."

"Well, paint me red and call me embarrassed," Carl said. "I wasn't sure if he was a hair dresser or maybe a singer with an album that would cheer her up."

"When in doubt, buy shoes," I told him, patting his arm. "At least where Mom's concerned. I prefer books, coffee, and comfortable t-shirts if Ben ever asks."

"Sign me up for chocolate and keep it coming," Monica said.

"And you, young lady?" Carl asked Grace. "What do you indulge in when you're feeling down?"

"Something salty like popcorn, and cozy blankets."

Leopold barked from the living room and came running in. He skittered around our feet and jumped up on Grace's legs.

"Down, now!" Carl said, grabbing the pudgy wiggle worm. "There's a good boy."

"I don't mind," Grace said, reaching over for Leopold. "I miss my dog." She picked him up and squeezed him while he licked her face and made excited snorty sounds.

"He likes you," Carl said. "Let's all go in and sit down."

We strode into the living room where Mom and Dad sat, Dad now across the room in an oversized chair sipping a drink. Mom stood and rushed over to Grace. "I'm so sorry. I know she was proud of the work you did for her. She trusted you completely with my wedding plans. I'm going to miss her so much."

Panic struck my chest. "Mom? Um... Mom?"

Monica looked like she'd swallowed her tongue and was having a hard time breathing.

"What are you talking about?" Grace asked, backing away from Mom. "You sound like... is Cecelia..."

Mom's eyes darted to mine. "Didn't you tell her?"

"We thought it would be a good idea to do it here with all of us."

Dad stood up. "We better make that two pairs of Jimmy's, Carl. I'll go with you."

"Tell me what's going on!" Grace looked from one of us to the next. Leopold whined in her arms.

"Grace," I said, "Cecelia's dead."

"How? I don't understand!"

Mom took the dog from her and set him on the floor, then ushered Grace to the sofa and sat beside her. We told her what we knew about Cecelia's passing.

"She was murdered?" Grace wrapped her arms around herself. "I need to go home."

"Is there anyone we can call for you?" I asked. "Your mom or dad? A sister or brother? Cousin? Anyone you would like to meet you at the airport?"

"No, it's just me." She bolted to her feet. "I need to go. I have to get home."

"Hang on," Dad said. "I'd want to get out of town too, if I were you, but the police will probably want to ask you some questions about Cecelia to try to figure this all out."

"I can call Ben and see if he can talk to you now, if you want," I said. "That way maybe you can catch a flight later tonight."

"I..." Grace crumpled to the floor in sobs. "I don't know what to do." Leopold rushed to her, nuzzling his way into her arms and licking the tears from her cheeks.

Monica got down on the floor next to her and put her arm around her shoulders. "I know this was a shock. It was for us, too. Cecelia needs us to find out who did this to her. That can only happen if we know everything there is to know about what was going on in her life and why someone would do this."

I lowered myself on the other side of Grace, knowing it would take a herculean effort to get me back up off the floor. "We can wait until you're ready to talk, but there must be a connection between Cecelia and Pastor Sonya if Cecelia was in her house. Whatever their connection was, it has to be the reason they were both killed."

Mom knelt in front of Grace and brushed some stray hairs away from her forehead. "Why don't we get you settled on the couch? It's been a lot to take in."

"I'm making popcorn," Carl said, swooping in with a fuzzy fleece blanket. "This should help."

"I'm heading over to the cafe for coffee for Cam, and chocolate for Monica," Dad said. "Any requests?"

I'm sure we were all thinking the same thing, that it was nice to offer, but nothing would really help. It was pretty clear that Dad and Carl needed something to do though to feel useful, so Mom said she wanted a chai tea and Grace said a Coke would be good. Once Dad left and Carl disappeared into the kitchen making popcorn, we situated ourselves on the sofa and loveseat, Grace with the blanket and Leopold, and me with Spook the cat on my lap wondering when he'd sneaked in.

"I don't know anything," Grace said. "All I knew was that she was looking forward to the wedding and to spending some time with an old friend."

"When you got here yesterday afternoon, you said she was stressed and not in good health," I said. "What did you mean by that?"

Grace shifted, pulling her legs underneath the blanket. "I think she was sick. She never told me, but she had a lot of doctor's appointments. She had me chasing down payments from clients a lot even if they weren't overdue, so I have the feeling she owed a lot of money. Maybe to doctors?"

"Could be." I looked over at Mom. "Do you know anything about Cecelia being sick?"

"No. She did complain about being fatigued quite often, but I figured that came with her career and her age. Vitamin D levels tend to fall in women our age."

My cell phone rang. It was Ben. I excused myself and took the call outside. After I answered he asked, "Have you seen Cecelia's assistant today?"

"She's here at the castle with us. I told her you would want to question her about Cecelia before she leaves town."

"She can't leave town. She's the only person other than your parents who knows the woman you found dead this morning. That makes her a potential suspect."

"And my parents?"

"Do they have an alibi for last night?"

"You know Mom was with me and Monica depending on the time. I'm not sure where Dad was."

He'd given me a way to ease into finding out the times of death.

"Walter put the time of death between six and eight PM last night for both women. That could change with the autopsies, but it's a good ballpark."

Walter Keene was the coroner. He was an older gentleman who knew his stuff and wasn't too tight lipped to share. He knew my team and I did good work and didn't complain about our involvement.

"I can ask Dad where he was, or let you do it when you see him at home. Unless you're going to call everyone in for questioning."

"No need to do that yet. Informality is the best way to get people talking at this point."

"And I'm sure you don't suspect my parents of murder, anyway."

He didn't respond to that statement.

"Ben? You don't think my dad killed either of them, do you?"

"Everyone's a potential suspect until I can rule them out, Cameron. You know that's my job. We've been around and around about this."

"But, *my dad?*"

"I don't personally think he killed her, but as a cop, I need an alibi."

"I'll give you an alibi--right in your rear end!"

"Cam--"

"I have to go console my mother whose friend was killed. I'll tell her how lucky she is to have an alibi for last night and not be on her son-in-law's list of potential murderers!"

"Cam!"

"Goodbye, Ben. See you later." I hung up and shoved my cell phone in my pocket. I didn't know if my reaction was justified or if I was overreacting. Clearly, Ben had a job to do and procedures to follow. Those procedures didn't exclude friends and family. They never did, and they never would, and it would continue to be an obstacle between us if I let it. He couldn't change it, so I would need to be the one to change how I felt about him suspecting everyone we knew or were related to.

For the time being, I needed to get my team together and make a plan for the vigil. There were too many gaps in the puzzle and I needed to start finding some pieces to put it together. Anna, Logan, Roy, and Johnna had been working on finding out who both of the women were--their histories and how they might have crossed paths. Before Ben came home and got wind of our part in putting the vigil together and figured out what it really was--a big distraction to get into that house--the Action Agency needed to meet and get our story straight and ducks in a row.

10

After Dad came back with my coffee I let him know that I had to go and that Ben would probably not be home until late so he didn't need to worry about buying steaks to cook out. Carl offered to take him to the Cornerstone and get him the best chicken dinner this side of Barberton, Ohio, the city known as the Fried Chicken Capital of America.

I'd already alerted the troop in our group text message, telling them to meet at my house. Anna and Logan always made sure Roy and Johnna got the message, as texts weren't the most reliable way for them to communicate, but they were a quick and private way for me to call them all together.

I got back to Ellsworth House, Ben's ancestral home that we inherited from his parents, just after five PM to find Old Dan in a lawn chair beside my bee house chatting away.

"Talking to the bees?" I asked him.

Old Dan was the oldest person in our town and he'd built my bee house and moved the hives the bees had constructed in my porch columns. He told me I had to talk to the bees and tell them what was going on in town or they'd swarm. I was pretty good at remembering to give them the gossip, but hadn't gotten around to the latest turn of events.

"I know you been busy with the two ladies who'd met their end, so I came to make sure your colony was up to date."

"I appreciate that, and I know they like to hear from you. Have you been singing to them?"

"I was just about to."

"How about some iced tea?"

"I wouldn't refuse some." He gave me a grin with missing teeth.

I ran inside and got a glass of iced tea for him and carried it back out. He was singing an old hymn and I sat on the porch steps to listen. His voice was husky and rusty and cracked a bit, but he carried a good tune.

When he finished, he took a long drink of tea and wiped his forehead. "Hot one today."

"It is. I've spent it inside, though. I don't suppose you know much about the pastor at the new church?"

"Pastor Sonya? Well, I know she came from Florida. She has family who still lives there I believe."

"How do you know so much about her?" I knew Old Dan didn't attend the new church. None of our older residents did.

"Elaina gets all the dirt on people," he said, chuckling. "You know how she is."

Elaina Nelson was one year younger than Old Dan. They'd gone to school together in a one-room schoolhouse that sat next door to me and was now an antique shop. They became a couple last year and together knew enough about this town and everyone in it to be dangerous.

"How did she find out about Pastor Sonya?" I asked.

"She has her ways. I don't question it."

Since my mother-in-law attended the new church the information might have come from her. I'd much rather get the lowdown from Old Dan than Mean Irene.

"There's a vigil tonight, huh? I was thinking of stopping over to pay my respects."

"It's at eight o'clock. Do you know where the pastor lived?"

"I believe so. I'm sure Elaina will want to tag along."

"I hear there should be a nice turn out."

"I'm sure you and your crew will want to snoop around while you're there. If there's anything Elaina and I can do to help, you just holler."

I leaned forward. "To tell you the truth, we'll need a distraction. Someone was searching for something in that house and we want to see if we can find out what."

"A distraction?" He scratched his chin. "I'm sure we can whip up something. Elaina's good with crowds and she sure was looking forward to going to that wedding tonight."

"Mom and Carl will reschedule. Any help you can give us tonight would be appreciated."

"It's the least we can do." He pushed himself up out of the folding chair, picked it up and gave me a wave. "We'll see you later."

I collected his iced tea glass from where he'd sat it beside the bee box in the grass, and watched him hobble off to his ancient green, bulbous pickup truck with the wooden side rails in the back. It started with a puff of smoke and a rattle, and off he went, down the road along the canal.

There were two beings in this town that Metamora couldn't survive without. One was Old Dan, and the other was Metamora Mike, the town duck. Mike was swimming with his three ducklings alongside him, full grown now, but still taking advantage of their dad's popularity to get breadcrumbs tossed their way.

Mike had to be as old as Old Dan, and had reached mythical status. There were even t-shirts with a cartoon of him on the pocket sold in some of the shops.

The high-pitched hum of Johnna's bright red electric scooter droned through the air. She was cruising along the canal road as fast as her four wheels would carry her with her knitting bag in the basket on the front. When it was nice out, she liked to ride in her mobility scooter instead of her car. She didn't need the scooter to get around, she walked just fine, but she used it like some older people used golf carts to get around in more upscale communities.

I went inside and got a pot of coffee brewing, made sure we had enough iced tea, and put some cookies on a plate on the table. The dogs were out in the backyard chasing each other through the sprinkler, and Mia was upstairs in her bedroom judging by the faint sound of music coming from above. I checked their water bowls on the patio and made sure they were full. Gus ran over and nudged me with a giant, wet head. The twin terrors couldn't be bothered to stop their mad dash through the water. Little Liam was nowhere to be found, so had to be upstairs with Mia, his one true love.

Back inside, I hustled upstairs before Johnna got off her scooter and came up the sidewalk. "Mia?" I called, knocking on her bedroom door. "Is Liam in there with you?"

Her door flew open and she stood there in a bikini holding her little puff of white fur. "He's right here. We're going to lay out and get a tan."

"I saw the other dogs outside having a blast in the sprinkler."

"They were rowdy and driving me crazy, so I gave them some outside time."

"We'll have to dry them off before they come inside, and make sure they aren't muddy."

"I know," she said, and rolled her eyes.

"Johnna, Roy, Anna, and Logan are on their way."

"Have fun with that. Can I go to a movie with Steph later?"

"As long as you're home by curfew and don't see anything rated R."

"I know, I know."

A movie would keep both of them away from the vigil. The less family I had involved, the better. I already had to get an alibi for one of them.

The doorbell rang. "There's Johnna," I said, and turned and ran down the steps.

Roy pulled in the driveway as Johnna stepped inside. "How's he doing?" I asked her while he was out of earshot. "Still off the booze?"

"He is," she said. "Some days are harder than others, but he wants to do it, so he's pushing through." She looked out the door at him. "The old goat."

"He's lucky to have someone like you to help him get through it."

She ambled by me. "He's lucky I haven't put rat poison in his coffee."

"I guess that murder wouldn't be a hard one to solve."

I waited at the door for Roy while Johnna got seated at the table. He ran across the yard in a jerky, animated way and took the porch steps two at a time. "Whoa, how much caffeine have you had today?" I asked him.

"I'm on a continuous cycle of coffee, tea, and anything with sugar. Speaking of, let me in Cameron Cripps Hayman. I require sustenance."

He rushed to the table, grabbed a handful of cookies, and started shoving them in his mouth.

"I'll get you that coffee," I said, rounding the counter and opening the cupboard door.

Mia traipsed down the steps with a long t-shirt over her swimsuit and flip flops on her feet. Liam followed on her heels. She had a small white box in her hand. "Mr. Lancaster," she said, "I figured you'd be over here soon and I heard you're off the whiskey and on a sugar high, so I brought some fudge home for you from the Soda Pop Shop."

"Bless your heart," he said, taking the box of fudge. "Now there's a nice, thoughtful young lady for you."

"Unlike, who?" Johnna said, raising her eyebrows.

"I won't speak unkindly about our Miss Smarty Pants and her holier than thou attitude lately, like nobody ever went to college before."

"Have a nice meeting," Mia said, dodging Roy on her way to the back door and outside with the dogs.

"Mia's a Daughter of Metamora," Johnna said. "She knows good manners."

"That was pretty nice of her," I said. Sometimes Mia surprised me.

She was a good kid as far as teenagers went, and had gotten so independent lately, I hardly saw her anymore. It would've been nice to have that wedding to spend time together as a family.

"Anna's not being any more of a smarty than normal," Johnna told Roy. "I think it's you who has a problem with her leaving to go to school. She's always been a little special to you."

"A special pain in my side," he grumbled.

I handed him his coffee and he took a big gulp that would've scorched my mouth.

The front door opened and Logan and Anna came inside. "We're not late are we?" Anna asked.

"Just in time," I said. "I have some good news about tonight. Elaina and Old Dan are going to cause a distraction so we can find a way inside Pastor Sonya's house."

"What part of that is good?" Roy asked. "Those two won't do nothin' but ensure we get busted."

"Elaina Nelson?" Anna's mouth dropped open. "You're trusting this operation to Elaina Nelson?"

"This is a mistake," Roy said. "There was already a movie called *Dumb and Dumber*, we don't need to remake it."

"Elaina can be resourceful when you point her in the right direction," Johnna said, pointing with her knitting needle. "But I don't trust Old Dan's sense of direction."

Logan had been tapping in numbers on his laptop keypad and stopped. "You don't want to know the odds of this working."

"Practically non-existent?" Roy asked.

"Pretty much," Logan confirmed.

"Listen guys, it's all we have. Two of us need to search one room, two another, and one the room that Monica and I didn't get to. Monica can be our lookout. With all of us in the house, we need someone on the outside keeping everyone looking the other way. Old Dan and Elaina offered to help and I took them up on it."

"We should start praying now," Johnna said. "Light some candles."

I was keeping a confident facade, but inside I knew it would take more than prayer, we were talking miracles for us to pull this off.

11

Police tape wrapped around Pastor Sonya's yard, front and back. I pulled the car off to the side of the road just past her house.

"We can't even get in the driveway?" Roy asked. "Where are you plannin' to have this vigil? In the street?"

We'd all crammed into my car. Monica in the passenger seat, Roy behind me, Johnna in the middle of the backseat, Logan behind Monica with Anna sitting on his lap. It wasn't the safest, but they all felt one escape car would be best.

"I'm not sure," I said. "Maybe the neighbors will let us use their yard."

Johnna craned her neck around to look out the back window. "Seeing as how there are already a group of people standing in the neighbor's yard, I don't think they have a choice."

"Dad's over there," Monica said. "And he has a pastor stole around his neck."

"Where on earth did he get that?" I asked.

"Probably came with the certificate," Roy said. "He did pay twenty bucks."

"Let's get over there and start this party," I said.

We piled out looking like a clown car at the circus and grabbed the boxes of candles from the trunk.

"Wish I had my scooter," Johnna said.

"It's one house down the road, and I'm carryin' your yarn and sticks," Roy said. "I'm the one should be complainin' seein' as I have no coffee in my hand." He yelled to me behind him, "Who was supposed to be in charge of refreshments at this shindig? I don't see a snack table."

"There are no refreshments," Anna said. "We stand and sing and pray, it's not a picnic."

"It's not a picnic," Roy repeated in a mocking voice. "You know everything."

"Stop being mean to her!" Logan shouted. "I've had enough."

Roy turned around. "Oh, big man are ya? Protecting your lady?"

Johnna whacked Roy in the shoulder. "Knock it off, you old fart. Don't be angry with them for doing something you never did."

"Can we have this out another time?" I asked. "We're in the middle of putting on a vigil at the moment."

"I figured this was your doing," Ben said, stepping out between two police SUV's at the end of the driveway."

"What gave it away?" Monica asked. "Dad over there preaching?"

Ben chuckled, even though I knew he was perturbed. "That tipped me off."

"Ain't nothing illegal about a private vigil," Roy said.

"Let's keep it that way," Ben said. "I don't want any of you putting one toe on this property, do you hear me?"

"Well, I don't have my hearing aids in, but I think I got it," Johnna said, smirking.

They continued walking, but I stayed behind to talk to Ben. "Are the cars parking on the side of the road going to be a problem?"

"Not for me."

"Did you grab anything for dinner?"

"Reins ran down to McDonalds."

"Mia's at a movie with Steph. You can join us for the vigil if you can spare a few minutes."

"I have a feeling I'll be out here before it's over."

"What does that mean?" I had a feeling I'd just been insulted. Although, we were planning a distraction to get him and the other police officers out of the house, so maybe it wasn't insulted that I felt, but annoyed that he'd anticipated our reason for being there.

"Wherever you and your Action Agency are, trouble follows."

"That's not true. We've put together a lot of nice events for this town. This vigil will be on that nice list."

"Tell it to Santa. I know you too well." He chuckled and leaned over to kiss my cheek. "A vigil is a nice idea. I'm sure everyone will appreciate it, but please, for my sanity, don't do anything you shouldn't."

Guilt seeped in through every pore on my body. I could only nod, knowing what I had planned, and felt like the worst person for lying. "I'll try," I added, to lessen the fib, but maybe that doubled it because I wouldn't try.

Of course he said not to do anything I shouldn't, and that was up to interpretation.

Ben headed back toward the house, and I continued on to the neighbor's yard where everyone was gathered. Cars were pulling over and parking on both sides of the street, and the group was getting larger by the second.

Logan and Anna passed out candles. Roy and Johnna chatted to a couple I didn't recognize, and Monica was standing with Dad.

Roy waved me over, and introduced me to Doris and Chuck the owners of the yard we were hijacking.

"We're happy to host," Doris said. "Pastor Sonya was a wonderful neighbor and it's a terrible loss. I didn't know the other woman, but what an awful thing to happen. I can't imagine who would do that."

"We weren't home when it happened," Chuck added. "Came home to find a bunch of cop cars over there and the house taped off. We'd heard about Pastor Sonya, of course. News gets around fast. But, do you have any idea who the other lady was?"

"No," I said, shooting Roy and Johnna a severe look. We didn't need to let that cat out of the bag just yet. "I was hoping you would have some information about that. "You weren't home though? So you didn't see anything?"

They both shook their heads. "I gave the police the login information from the camera on our doorbell," Chuck said. "I didn't see anything on there, but if they can find anything they're welcome to it."

"Can you show me?" I asked. "It's just that I was the one who found the woman in Pastor Sonya's house. My sister and I stopped by to see if she had any pets inside that might need caring for and found the woman inside. I feel like I should try to do whatever I can to help the police figure out what happened."

"How terrible for you," Doris said. "We'll show you the footage. Chuck can bring it up on his cell phone."

"Here we go," Chuck said, logging into the app for his doorbell on his phone. He tapped the screen then handed it to me to watch. Roy and Johnna leaned in on both sides of me.

I didn't see anything other than cars driving by. The video showed the corner of Pastor Sonya's front yard, but not as far as her driveway, so anyone who turned in wouldn't be recorded.

"Is there a way for you to email this to me?" I asked, thinking that Logan might have a way to enhance the video or evaluate it frame by frame.

"I suppose it wouldn't hurt to have more eyes on it," he said. "Only promise to tell the police if you find something, okay?"

"I promise," I said, and gave him my email address. "Do you have any other cameras in the back of the house?"

"No, only the doorbell. That's as fancy as we get."

"And that took us forever to figure out," Doris said, laughing.

"I'm still trying to figure out how to set the clock in my car," I said. "A doorbell camera is way beyond me."

"This is quite the turn out," Chuck said.

I turned around to find their entire front yard filled with people. There were way more than fifty. Word must've spread to the rest of the congregation through the prayer team who we contacted.

Dad stood on a wooden milk crate that he got from somewhere

with his hands raised. Fortunately, Reverend Stroup stood on the ground beside him, ready to assist if needed.

"Thank you all for coming out tonight," Dad said, loud enough to get everyone's attention. "I'm Brother Joe, ordained by the monks of The Bottom of the Mountain Monastery in Nepal. My daughter, the organizer of tonight's vigil, has asked me to lead us in song and prayer. Please bow your heads."

"Bottom of the Mountain is right," Roy muttered. "Bottom of the barrel more like."

Johnna snickered.

"Bow your heads," I whispered to them.

Dad said a prayer about death and the afterlife that I was certain he made up on the spot. Admittedly, it wasn't terrible. He might actually pull this off.

"As the sun is setting," Dad continued after the prayer, "let us light our candles and sing to the spirits in the twilight."

"Spirits in the twilight?" Johnna smacked her leg and laughed.

Dad started singing Amazing Grace and everyone joined in. The flames of all the candles flickering in the dusk looked like fireflies. Voices rose and fell with the chorus and there was a real sense of community and coming together, and even worship. Apparently, a theology-degreed leader and sitting under a church roof weren't necessary to call up the holy spirit. I should've known that in my heart already and not doubted Dad's ability to lead a group of people in prayer and song.

Across the mass of people, I spotted Irene and Stewart standing with my mom and Carl. Irene didn't look pleased, but she'd get over it. Grace stood beside Mom, and she had Leopold on a leash. He was a good dog who'd really taken a liking to Grace. He didn't seem interested in finding his way to his house though, which I thought was strange.

I hadn't seen any dog toys or anything inside the house, but I hadn't been looking for them either. They could've been in the room where we found Cecelia, or in the bedroom we didn't go into. If we got inside tonight, I'd see what I could find of Leopold's and grab it.

We sang two more songs and it was completely dark out. Doris and Chuck turned on the lamp post beside the end of their driveway and combined with the candles a warm glow illuminated everyone's faces.

I almost forgot about our ulterior motive for being there. But the roar of an engine and a husky, rusty voice over a loud speaker brought me back to my senses.

"Here comes the bride!" Old Dan's voice blared out from the speaker mounted on top of his truck. The vintage Chevy rumbled into view. Elaina stood in the back dressed in a bridal gown with a veil pulled over her face.

"That's going to get everybody's attention, all right," Roy said.

"She didn't ask me to knit her something blue." Johnna huffed and folded her arms.

"They're not actually getting married are they?" I asked, certain my eyes and ears were deceiving me.

"You asked for a distraction, Cameron Cripps Hayman, and you got it."

12

"Here comes the bride!" Old Dan called, grinning ear-to-ear.

Elaina was wedged between the cab of the truck and a stack of hay bales. She waved like Princess Di and blew kisses to the crowd.

"Pastor, will you marry us with these good people to witness?" Old Dan asked.

Dad looked to Reverend Stroup who pointed to his throat. Dad then turned to Old Dan and said, "Why not? I am ordained, so something else to cross off my bucket list."

Old Dan let out a whoop and parked the truck right in the middle of the road. Looking closer, I realized there were bouquets of flowers attached to the wooden rails on the bed of the pickup and the bridal bouquet looked awfully familiar.

"Those are Mom's flowers!" Monica said. "Can you believe this?"

"Well, she wasn't using them."

"They brought food!" Roy shouted. "And coffee! Hallelujah!"

Old Dan had gotten some of the men in the crowd to help him unload the pickup that was filled with a couple folding tables and boxes of foil covered trays of food from the caterer and a large stainless steel coffee urn. Next came the cake, and last came Elaina.

"It's everything from Mom and Carl's wedding," Monica said, sounding like she was going to cry. "We put so much effort into picking all of that out. We put up with so much from Mom."

I put an arm around her shoulder. "The bridezilla has spoken and passed the torch to Grandma Diggity."

As a silent partner in Monica's dog boutique, Elaina had given herself what she said was a young and hip nickname.

Monica sighed. "I know we'll have to do it all again when they reschedule, but I'm going to need a long vacation first."

"Let's go help them set up before our disappearing act."

We made our way through the crowd to where the tables were being set up. Dad was introducing Old Dan and Elaina to Chuck and Doris. "I'm sorry to impose on you like this," Old Dan was saying. "Friends of ours had to cancel their ceremony and we didn't want everything to go to waste."

"A vigil and now a wedding," Doris said. "I can't think of a better way to honor Pastor Sonya and I hear the other woman was a wedding planner. It's a fitting tribute to them both."

"I guess details about Cecelia are spreading fast," I whispered to Monica.

"I heard someone mention she was from Orlando," Monica said. "So misinformation is spreading, too."

"Orlando? Maybe she did live there before LA. I know she lived somewhere that started with an O."

Mom, Grace, and Irene set out paper plates, napkins, and plastic silverware. "This was nice of you, Mom."

"Anything to help," she said, giving me a sly wink. Old Dan must've filled them in on the plan.

"Planning the vigil was a generous thing to do," Irene said to me. "I'd like it if you would involve me in anything that requires the help of my prayer team in the future."

"Absolutely," I said. "Will do." I wouldn't be surprised if she expected me to bow and kiss her ring. "Have you talked to Ben? He's inside Pastor Sonya's house."

"I called and let him know his father and I were out here. He said he'd come out in a few minutes to say hello."

That was perfect. If Ben was out here, we could sneak inside. He might wonder where we were, but hopefully we could get back out and blend with the crowd before he had any suspicions about us doing something we shouldn't as he put it.

"I'm sure he won't want to miss the wedding," I said.

My cell phone vibrated in my pocket. I stepped away from Irene and the wedding prep to check it. There was a text message in the Action Agency chat.

Me and Smart Girl are sneakin' around back to take a look. Fiddlesticks and Computer Kid are followin' in 10. We'll send the call clear for Mrs. Fuzz and Sis. Too many eyes on ya to be gone long. Over and out - Capt'n Eagle Eye

Capt'n Eagle Eye? All the coffee was making Roy nuttier than normal, and Ben wouldn't be very pleased with the cop jab with calling me Mrs. Fuzz. Good thing he'd never know about it. I'm not sure how the secret names would hide the fact that the message was on my phone in a text chat with all five of us, but I couldn't fault Roy for being inventive.

Monica came up alongside me. "Where's the rest of the team?"

I showed her the message. "They're getting the party started."

"Sis? That's the best he could come up with for me? That's lame."

"I'm Mrs. Fuzz, so I don't want to hear it."

"He's going to have to do much better than that if we're getting nicknames."

"Stay close so I can tell you when it's time for us to join in the fun."

"I don't know why you don't just add me to the text chat."

"You can deny any knowledge of anything we put in there. It's for your own good."

"You have teenagers in that chat," she said. "Try again."

"Yeah, yeah. I'll add you."

Old Dan rolled a red carpet right down the middle of the road. His son, Frank, put up orange cones to block traffic in both directions. I recognized this as another diversion since it was insane to make a wedding aisle in the road instead of the yard, and it would be sure to draw out the police.

"Everyone, line the aisle," Dad said from the truck's loudspeaker, "and we'll get started with the ceremony."

The crowd of people still with their candles lit, made their way like a glowing wave across the yard to the road. The first car pulled up behind the orange cones and the driver got out, looking more than a little confused.

"I can't believe they're getting married," I said. "That's taking this distraction thing a little far."

"I'm not surprised," Monica said. "Elaina has her hooks in that man and she's not letting go. You're never too old for love."

"They'll probably outlive us all. Those two and Mike."

"Is that Mom's wedding dress?" Monica tilted her head to the side, examining the gown.

"Can't be. Elaina's probably had it in storage for decades waiting to pull it out."

Old Dan and Frank stood at the bed of the pickup with Dad while Elaina was ushered to the end of the aisle by Mom and Irene. "Who will give this woman away?" Dad asked.

"Wait! I will!" came a shout from down the road. I squinted my eyes into the dark to find Steph and Mia running for all they were worth to make it on time. Steph was wearing Mia's bridesmaid dress. "I'll give my great-grandma away!" Steph called.

"We'll wait for you, dear," Dad said. "Don't twist your ankle in those shoes."

In front of us, Carl turned around and asked, "Are those Jimmy Chews?"

"No, Carl," I said, chuckling.

Out of the corner of my eye, I saw Johnna tuck her arm into Logan's and steer him in the opposite direction from the wedding. "Team two is going in," I whispered to Monica.

"This is starting to feel like I'm part of Seal Team Six or something," she said. "I'm getting nervous. My hands are sweating."

A horn blasted behind Elaina and the orange cones at her end of the aisle. A semi-truck sat with its stack belching and the driver glaring at the blocked road.

Another car pulled up behind the one stopped at Dan's truck and honked. The first car's driver had joined in the wedding guests and was eating cheese and crackers. He waved at the driver who honked behind his parked vehicle. "It's a wedding! Might as well come wait it out. There's a shrimp platter!" He grabbed a piece and dangled it in front of his face as evidence.

"Well, that ought to do it," I said, watching the front door of Pastor Sonya's house for Ben, Reins and the rest of the cops inside.

The semi's horn blared again and the driver hung out his window. "Get this mess off the road! I have a load to deliver!"

Elaina turned on him and held her fist in the air. "So help me if you ruin my wedding day!"

"You'll do what?" the truck driver yelled.

"Come down here and I'll turn you over my knee young man!" She waved her fist and her veil shifted, blowing out to the side. One of the guests' candles lit the end of the netting on fire.

"You're on fire!" The truck driver screamed.

"You haven't seen me angry yet!" Elaina shouted back.

"No! You're on fire!"

Someone in the crowd tackled her to the ground and rolled her up in the end of the red carpet, pulling off the veil and patting the fire out, all the while Elaina screamed and kicked thinking she was being attacked.

"What in the Sam Hill is going on out here?" Ben yelled, running into Doris and Chuck's yard. Reins and a couple other officers were close behind.

"That's our cue," I told Monica and the two of us backed our way out of the glow of the wedding goers' candles and into the darkness surrounding the house.

"Run," Monica whispered, and took off, leaving me to jog along behind. I'm not a runner. My knee won't allow it. Neither will my lungs. Even my teeth protest when I attempt it. If there's ever a zombie outbreak I'll be the first person eaten and I've made my peace with that.

We ducked under the crime scene tape and scrambled to the back door through the pitch black to find my crew was still standing outside. "What are you waiting for?" I asked, panting and holding a stitch in my side.

"Are they out of the house?" Anna asked.

"Yes!"

"You're supposed to text us when they come out," Johnna said.

"That's not what I was told!"

"What were you told?" Logan asked.

"Does it matter now?" Roy asked. "Let's get in there."

"Last time he's in charge of communication," Johnna said.

"Stop griping and get your compression sox moving into the house," Roy said.

"What was Elaina screaming about?" Anna asked, as we started in through the back door.

"Sounded like an alien abduction," Roy said.

"She caught on fire," I told them. "Candles and netting don't mix well."

Johnna harrumphed. "You can't have a wedding with nothing blue and expect nobody to catch fire."

"I'll have to remember that one," Monica said, tiptoeing in behind me.

Roy crossed the kitchen and headed down the hallway giving tactical hand signs, which I deciphered to mean he and Johnna would check out the room on the right at the back that Monica had been in when we found Cecelia. Anna and Logan would check out the room where I found her, and Monica would check out the third room we hadn't been in. I was put on watch detail at the front window.

Being relegated to look out wasn't my first choice, but it did give me the perk of watching the wedding fiasco going on outside.

I stood to the side of the window and peeked from behind the heavy curtain. Elaina was back on her feet--bare feet now--without the veil. Her white hair stood on end and looked like a scrub brush used to wash dishes.

She held one white patent leather flat and was searching the ground for the other. If she had to go down the aisle without something patent leather, which was her trademark, I couldn't imagine the fallout. Mia and Steph helped, and the truck driver actually found it behind one of his front eighteen wheels. He seemed to have calmed down ever since she caught fire.

Ben was talking to Old Dan, probably trying to get him to move his truck. Dad held the CB that broadcast over the speaker, and I could hear him calling for order, and banging his Bible on the hood of the truck like a judges gavel. Reverend Stroup was doing his darndest to get the Bible from Dad. Banging the Good Book on a truck hood has to be blasphemous even if his intention was sound.

It was pandemonium in the street, and exactly what we needed.

"That room's totally empty," Monica said, joining me at the window. "Not one piece of furniture or one thing hung in the closet. What's going on out there?"

"What's not going on out there?" I said, laughing. "Oh, look, two more cars just pulled up in the line on the street."

Reins ended up taking the crime tape down from in front of Pastor Sonya's driveway and letting cars turn around while Ben tried to get Old Dan's truck moved.

"Let them marry! Let them marry!" Dad started chanting in the loudspeaker. The crowd joined in, and Ben held his hands up and backed away. Dad gave him the thumbs up sign and said, "We'll be quick. Then you and the other cops here tonight can join us for cake."

"Ben's going to be so mad at Dad," Monica said. "Have fun with that."

"I just don't want to be on that list," I said. "I hope they're hurrying back there."

"I'll go see."

Monica dashed back down the hallway and I continued my watch. One of Reins's officers was setting up flares in the road to warn travelers of the stop ahead.

The bridal march began to ring out over the loudspeaker. Dad left Reverend Stroup in charge of the music and hustled back around to the tailgate of the truck where Old Dan and Frank stood.

At the end of the aisle, Steph tried to flatten Elaina's hair and gave up. She handed her the bouquet, which was missing about half of its flowers and what was left were smashed.

Elaina gave her great-granddaughter a kiss on the cheek, waved at Steph's sister Leann and the girls' mom, Sue, standing near Old Dan, and she headed down the aisle arm-in-arm with Steph.

She only got distracted twice on her way down the aisle. Once by a shiny gold bow that had blown off one of the floral arrangements tied to the back of the truck. She picked it up and tucked it in the Brillo of hair on top of her head. The second time was to polish a black smudge off the toe of her shoe with her sleeve.

Each time Old Dan laughed and called her back to her task. The pair of them really were good for each other. She'd brought him out of his shell, and he kept her somewhat on the rails.

Being so caught up in the wedding, I missed that two of Sheriff Reins's men were heading back down the driveway. I didn't know if they were intending to come back inside yet, but we couldn't risk it.

"Ravioli!" I whisper shouted. "Ranunculus! Rhubarb!"

We had a code word for times like this, but nobody could ever remember what it was. "They're coming!"

"They're here," said a man's voice behind me.

13

My stomach dropped and I spun around to find another officer standing there.

"What are you doing in here," he asked, "and who's with you?"

"Just me," Monica said, coming down the hall. "We found Pastor Sonya's dog at the church. She must've brought him with her when she... We wanted to see if he had any bowls or a bed or toys. Have you found anything like that?"

"You trampled all over a crime scene to find dog supplies?" he asked.

I shrugged. "We knew you were all too busy to bother with it."

"No, there's no evidence that she had any pets. Now leave before I take you to the Brookville jail for further questioning."

"Okay," I said. "We're sorry."

Monica and I hustled out the back door. "What are the others going to do?" she asked.

I nodded to the end of the house. "There's our answer."

Johnna was stuffed through the window, her bottom half wriggling to get free. We ran to help her the rest of the way out. Roy didn't hesitate to launch himself through, landing in a heap on the ground, groaning.

"Close the window," I told Monica, while I helped Roy up off the ground. "What's with you and shoving people in and out of windows, even yourself?"

"You coulda broken a hip, you old fool," Johnna said to him.

"I got us out, didn't I? Would you rather be arrested?"

Johnna just glowered at him. "I don't appreciate you man handling me."

"Trust me, lady, I had no pleasure in doing it."

"I'm glad we're out of the house," I said, "whatever the method. I don't know what Logan and Anna are going to do."

We stood around, pacing and trying to come up with a way to help them when not even two minutes later, they were unceremoniously kicked out the back door into the dark with us.

"How did you get out?" I asked.

Anna smirked. "Simple. We were making out when he came into the bedroom. He just figured we were some dumb teenagers who found a place to have some alone time and kicked us out."

"Did you manage to look around at all or were you lip locked the whole time?" Roy asked.

Anna whipped a manila folder out from under her shirt. "I think we need to look at this. It's financial records for the church and it's all we found before we had to improvise."

"I'll stow it in my knitting bag," Johnna said, taking it from her. "Nobody will look in there for any contraband."

"Let's split up so we don't all show up at the same time back in the wedding crowd."

Monica and I went all the way around to the far side of Doris and Chuck's house and joined the crowd at the end of the aisle. Roy ran right through the middle and made a beeline to the coffee urn with Johnna on his tail. Anna and Logan strolled through the yard holding hands like they didn't have a care in the world. Nobody would suspect any of us for just snooping through a crime scene, other than the officer who found us and fortunately, he didn't know me.

Elaina had made it down the aisle and I missed how it happened, but her beat up bouquet of flowers was down to only a nub of a white rose. She plucked it and tucked it in her hair along with the gold ribbon she'd collected a little farther back along the aisle. The plastic nosegay holder was tossed into the air in an arc behind her and bounced on the asphalt road.

"At least she's having a good time," Monica said. "I'm going to go see how Mom's doing watching her wedding paraphernalia get destroyed."

Grandma Diggity was just this side of senile, so everybody who knew her anticipated this spectacle as soon as the wedding was announced. Mom was newer to town, but she had to have known what an Elaina and Dan wedding would be like. I hoped she wasn't upset.

Steph put Elaina's hand in Old Dan's and gave him a kiss on the cheek. He said something to her that none of us could hear, and she smiled and stepped aside.

"Now then," Dad said, clearing his throat. There was no way he was prepared for that trip down the aisle. "We're gathered here this evening to celebrate the union of this man and this woman."

"I do!" Elaina shouted, and dove toward Old Dan with her lips puckered.

"I do, too," he said, chuckling, and braced himself for impact.

Their lips collided, and I'd bet anything that the few remaining teeth Old Dan had were no longer connected to his gums.

"I now pronounce you husband and wife," Dad said, closing his Bible. Reverend Stroup looked like his head was about to explode.

The crowd cheered and candles flickered and were dropped as everyone attempted to applaud while holding tapers. Fortunately, we had the storm the night before or the generosity of Pastor Sonya's neighbors would've been repaid by their yard going up in flames.

Ben came up beside me. "Nice wedding, huh?"

"Unexpected," I said, "but nice. It's good that Mom and Carl's food and flowers didn't have to go to waste."

"Speaking of your Mom, I don't think that dog she has belonged to Pastor Sonya. There wasn't any dog food or a leash in the house. Nothing that a dog owner would need."

I played dumb and pretended that I didn't know that already. "Really?Maybe she made her own food for him and he ate it off of a plate?"

"Still, no leash? Not a bone or a ball? No tie out? There's no fence."

"It does seem like there would be at least one thing to indicate she had a dog."

"He belongs to someone else. Your mom needs to know so she doesn't get too attached. Can you and Monica put up flyers in Dog Diggity and around town?"

"We'll do that right away. The poor guy probably misses his person. It's strange that Monica doesn't recognize Leopold considering every person who has a dog in Metamora brings theirs into her shop."

"I'd imagine there are some people who don't. It's treats and dog clothes, and not everyone spends that kind of money on their dog. A French Bulldog does cost a pretty penny though, so I wouldn't think whoever owns him would have a problem buying him expensive, hand-kitted sweaters."

"He might be a rescue," I said. "I just don't know what he was doing in the church."

Ben's eyes narrowed. I could tell he was forming a theory. "I'll see you at home later," he said, dashing any hope I'd had of him sharing his thoughts with me.

"You're not staying for cake?" I asked.

"Save me a piece. I gotta get back inside." He gave me a quick kiss and headed across the yard to Pastor Sonya's house.

I spotted Roy and Johnna at the cake table, circling like vultures, and made my way over to them. "Are you two ready to go? We should get back to my house and go over that file Anna nabbed."

"Have you lost your marbles?" Roy asked. "You're expectin' us to skedaddle before eatin' the cake?"

"There's a lot to unpack in this case. The dog didn't even belong to Pastor Sonya."

"I can only unpack after I pack in some cake," he said. "Sugar and caffeine, Cameron Cripps Hayman. Sugar and caffeine."

"You heard the man," Johnna said.

My crew had spoken, at least two of them. Since we'd ridden together, I couldn't leave without them no matter how much I might want to. I figured it wouldn't hurt to find Mom and let her know about Leopold before she got so attached she didn't want to let him go.

Poor, Mom. First the wedding was called off, and now the dog she took in had an owner out there somewhere. Mom wasn't having a good weekend.

THE CAKE HAD BEEN CUT. Elaina and Old Dan smashed the whole top of it into each other's faces, laughing and carrying on like a couple of middle school kids, and the crowd that had first gathered for a vigil and ended up as impromptu wedding guests was departing.

"Her entire head is buttercream," Johnna said, eyeing Elaina with a horrified stare. "That's never going to come out. She'll have to shave herself bald."

"Give 'erself a good old chrome dome," Roy said with a mouth full of white cake and icing.

Anna and Logan stood beside us. Anna had finished her dainty piece of cake, and Logan couldn't have any due to being gluten intolerant and allergic to chocolate.

I'd thought for sure he'd had cookies at my house before, but come to think of it, his fingers were always glued to his laptop keyboard.

Frank had tied aluminum cans to the back of Old Dan's truck and hung a sign that said just hitched. Dad was helping Reverend Stroup hoist Elaina up into the passenger side of the cab. She kept turning around to wave goodbye to everyone and they'd lose any leverage they'd gotten and have to start all over.

"Bet he's glad he came to town," Roy said, watching my dad and chuckling.

"He got to perform a wedding and a vigil on the same night," I said. "Where else can he do that?"

"Nowhere on this great, green earth," Johnna said. "This town's got a screw loose."

"Ain't never boring though, isn't that right, Miss Smarty Pants?" Roy asked Anna. "You're gonna be sorry when you leave here."

"I'll come back. My family lives here. It's not like I'm moving to Mars."

Johnna shook her head. "What he's trying to say is, he'll miss ya."

Roy put his plate down and tugged on the lapels of his ratty old navy blue sports coat. "Yeah, what she said."

Anna threw her hands in the air. "That's why you're being so mean to me?"

"He has trouble expressing his feelings," Johnna said. "Don'tcha Roy?"

He bobbed his head around and looked at his feet. "She's right. I'm gonna miss your nerd boy there, too. It won't be the same without ya."

"What's going on?" Anna asked.

"I told ya, I'm gonna miss ya. How many times do I need to say it?"

"No," she said, pointing over my shoulder. "Ben's arresting Chuck."

"The neighbor?" I spun around to see Ben putting handcuffs on Pastor Sonya's neighbor, the man who'd been such a good sport about us taking over his yard tonight.

"Well, ducks on a biscuit," Roy said. "I didn't see that coming."

"Neither did I."

"We need to get back to the house and read that file," I said. "Come on. Let's get out of here."

Monica came running over to join us as we were half way to the road. "Don't leave without me!"

"I knew you'd catch up. You run faster than me."

"Was this going to be payback for me taking off and running through the backyard earlier?"

"I hadn't thought of that, but now that you mention it, yes." I nudged her shoulder with mine. "We need to see if Leopold has a microchip. Does Quinn have one of those scanners?"

"I'll ask him. If so, we can use it tomorrow."

"Good, because he was left in that church and Ben thought there'd been someone else in there when Pastor Sonya was hanged. Whoever it was is probably Leopold's owner."

"Could it be that easy?"

"Probably not, but at least it was one thing we can accomplish. So far, this case is a lot of loose ends and no beginnings. If there isn't a clue in the file folder, I'm not sure where to look next."

14

The six of us sat around my kitchen table with the dogs barking and growling, playing tug of war and chasing each other through the house. We couldn't hear ourselves think.

"I needed to give them a walk," I said. "I've been gone most of the day and they're full of energy."

Dad wrangled my pack and herded them outside. "You can play chase out here. Run around until your hearts are content." He gave me and Monica both a hug. "It's been a long night. I'm turning in. You have a nice group of people in this town. A little bit off center, but they're all right."

"Off center's a nice way to put it," Roy said. "We're all whacky. Have to be to stick around here."

"Maybe so," Dad said, "but you all must have an interesting life living in this place."

"I suppose so."

Dad told everyone goodnight and disappeared upstairs to the spare room.

Back at the table, the crew was anxious to get started. "Okay, I said. Tell us about the file folder. It was in the room where I found Cecelia, right?"

"Right," Logan said, and glanced side-eyed at Anna.

"Actually," she said, "It was where the outline of her body was. Like she'd been laying on it."

"Was there blood?" Roy asked.

Johnna cringed, and I wasn't sure I wanted to know the answer, but we didn't have a cause of death yet, so it might help us on that end.

"No," Logan said. "Which means she was probably strangled or hit over the head."

"By Chuck next door?" Monica asked. "That's what doesn't make sense to me. What could he have to do with any of this? He couldn't have known Cecelia, could he?"

"Ben must've found something to link him," I said. "So far he's got more than we do."

Anna opened the file folder. "Let's see what Cecelia was after."

"The police are gonna be missing that," Roy said. "And they know the two of you we're in that bedroom."

"The officer that caught us didn't ask our names," Logan said, "so we can copy everything and drop the folder off somewhere anonymously for them to pick up."

"Somewhere without cameras," Johnna said. "They'll get you every time with those hidden cameras."

I almost laughed thinking about Johnna trying to shoplift yarn from Walmart and getting caught on the security cameras. If anyone knew about that, it was her.

"She knows of what she speaks," Roy said.

"Speaking of hidden cameras!" I pulled up my email on my phone. "I almost forgot. Chuck, the next door neighbor, has a doorbell with a camera. He sent me the video footage from the night of the murder. Logan, I'm going to send it to you to see what you can do with it."

"I'll give it my best shot," he said.

"This looks like it's all info on state requirements for a pre-school," Anna said shuffling through the papers in the file. "There's a list of regulations printed off a website," she flipped to the next sheet of paper in the pile, "there's a letter from the church board about fundraising," she turned to the next page, "and a bunch of receipts from a place called Education Equipment Ltd."

"What would she be buying there? Sounds like a place that sells projectors or desks or something," I said. "They're nowhere near the purchasing phase if they're just starting to fundraise."

"They aren't even fundraising yet," Anna said, whipping out another letter. "The board gave provisional approval pending further research into requirements for medical safety. They state here they don't feel adequate planning and documentation has been done in all areas of child safety and that they would review an updated proposal for the pre-school in six months. This is dated four weeks ago."

I grabbed a cookie to nibble. It helped me think. "Then why would there be payments made to Educational Equipment Ltd."

"Maybe it's church supplies." Monica said.

"No," Logan said, scrolling down his laptop screen. "It's not even an operational business that I can find. It's owned by Blue Horizons, LLC., and they own a bunch of other businesses."

"She was being scammed," Roy said.

"Why would she be paying them money in the first place?" Johnna asked. "And was she fundraising or not? Irene told me tonight that she volunteered to take over the fundraising for Pastor Sonya's pre-school project and they better let her since she already donated so much money to it."

"Irene gave Pastor Sonya money for the pre-school that the church board hadn't even approved yet?" I rubbed my forehead. "We're definitely on to something here. I just don't know what."

"What other businesses does Blue Horizons, LLC, own? Monica asked, leaning over to take a look at Logan's laptop screen.

"Looks like a tanning salon named Slo Glo, and one called Linen Supply House. Let me find the last one online.

He typed and hit enter. "Linen Supply house is straight forward. They rent linens. Tablecloths, napkins, runners, awnings, curtains."

"So two more businesses under this umbrella LLC?" I asked to verify the info.

"Correct," Logan said.

"Does it say where Blue Horizons, LLC is located?"

"Let me go back to the LLC search." Logan tapped away and then looked up. "Orlando, Florida."

"Orlando, Florida!" Monica and I shouted in unison--and so did Anna.

Outside, the dogs heard us and ran to the back door. They barked and pawed at the glass like they had to break through and save us.

"Oops," I said. "We alerted the troops. They think we're under attack."

"I'll grab some treats for them," Monica said.

"Will someone explain what's so important about Orlando?" Johnna asked.

"Monica heard one of the people at the vigil say that they heard that Cecilia was from Orlando. I knew she'd lived somewhere that started with an O before moving to LA."

Anna nodded. "Logan and I did some digging and she lived in Orlando before she went out to LA."

"And the dearly departed pastor was sending money to a fake company owned by a place in Orlando," Roy said, and clicked his tongue. "The plot is on foot."

"It's 'the game is afoot,'" Logan said.

Roy smirked. "A game is a game and a foot is a foot. I don't know how you got into that fancy school you're goin' to."

"No!" Anna laughed. "The saying is from Sherlock Holmes. The game is afoot. Not, the plot is on foot."

Roy wave his hand at her. "Don't believe everything you read."

"Blackmail?" Monica asked.

"Let's eliminate the logical first," Anna said. "Was Pastor Sonya ever married, or was she planning on getting married, or paying for a wedding? Maybe she owed Cecelia money and was paying it off through a fundraising scam."

"Roy and Johnna," I said, "I know it's only been twenty-four hours and those have been busy, but did either of you get any info on Pastor Sonya?"

"Sonya Billingsley has never married," Johnna said, pulling more yarn free from her knitting bag. "She wasn't dating anyone either. She was born in Cincinnati, Ohio, actually, went to college at Ohio State before seminary school at Trinity Divinity School."

"Ohio State? With Mom and Cecelia?" Monica said. She and I locked eyes, both wondering what Mom knew that she didn't realize she knew.

Monica grabbed her phone and dialed. While it rang, she drummed her fingers on the table. "Mom! In college did you know Sonya Billingsley?"

We watched, eyes locked on Monica while she listened to Mom's answer.

"No, not Beth Billingsley. Sonya, like Pastor Sonya." Monica glanced around the table at us.

Logan did some tapping on his keyboard. "According to Ancestry dot com, Beth is Sonya Billingsley's middle name. Born in Cincinnati."

"Mom!" Monica shouted. "Beth Billingsley *is* Pastor Sonya!"

I heard a lot of noise on the other end of the line, but couldn't make out what Mom was saying.

"I know you never saw her," Monica said. "I know. Your face was in Carl's shoulder when we found her... Yes, I'm sure it's her. Listen, we need to know how she could have been linked with Cecelia. Okay. Yes, call us back."

Monica hung up. The rest of us were leaning forward toward her, about ready to pounce on the table.

"Spit it out already!" Roy said.

"Okay, so Beth--Pastor Sonya--was in Mom and Cecelia's sorority. They didn't really hang out with her, but they were friends. Beth was a couple years older, and after she graduated, that's the last they saw of her. They didn't stay in touch since they weren't that close to begin with.

Mom and Carl were dropping Grace off at the Briar Bird. She's going to call back when she's home, but she said that's all she knows about her."

"Somebody's pickin' off old sorority chicks," Roy said. "This is the plot of a bad horror movie. *I Know What You Did Summer of '71.*"

"But it's not a horror movie," I said. "It's real. And two of Mom's sorority sisters are dead. That means she could be the next target."

~

I DID what any daughter would do in the same situation, I called my police officer husband and told him what was going on. I may have left out some details, forwarding right to the Ancestry dot com search that led us to Pastor Sonya's full legal name and how Mom realized she knew her and now there were two members of Mom's old sorority dead in Metamora on the same day.

Ben quickly came to the same conclusion that I had--Mom needed protection. He posted a cop to guard at the gatehouse of Hilltop Castle, and left his own K9 partner, Brutus, there as well. Quinn brought his K9, Conan, retired from the Garda Dog Unit in Ireland, to stay inside the castle with Mom and Carl. Leopold was a good dog, but not trained for this task.

Involving the police put a damper on the Action Agency's amateur investigation for the night. We decided to sleep on it and figure out what we knew and how it fit together in the morning.

Ben got home about twenty minutes after Mia, which was about an hour after my crew left the house. I was in bed doing my best to read, but my mind wouldn't focus on the words and before I knew it a chapter had gone by and I couldn't remember any of it.

"Don't worry," Ben said, crawling in bed on his side. "Hilltop Castle is a fortress."

Being that I'd saved Carl's life almost a year ago from someone he knew and trusted and let into the castle, it was only a fortress if someone didn't open the door.

I rolled on my side to face my stubborn resident police officer. "Ben, I need to know everything. I realize it's an open investigation, but this is my mom we're talking about. If her life is in danger, I need all the facts."

"You know I can't tell you--"

"You will tell me," I said sitting upright and staring down at him. "This is for better and for worse and it's about to get a lot worse if something happens to her. That means I'll make it worse for you if I could've done something to figure this all out and you didn't tell me everything."

He stared at the ceiling like a lifeline might suddenly fall from it. Then he sighed. "Fine. What do you want to know?"

"How is Chuck involved?"

"The neighbor?"

"You cuffed him next door tonight. Yes, the neighbor." I was in no mood for a verbal tango.

"I cuffed him to get him to talk, but he didn't give me anything. I found a voided check written to him for a lot of money. I thought it might be something, but turns out he did some drywall work for her and wouldn't accept the check when she gave it to him."

"How much money?"

"Fourteen hundred and some change."

"Her personal check or the church?"

"Church. We're verifying who owns the house, and I put in a request with the board for any contract with Pastor Sonya that might say if she was responsible for repairs or if the church footed the bill."

"Like a contract when they hired her saying if the house or utilities and repairs were part of the deal?"

"Yes. Religious professions don't pay a lot, so housing is often factored in."

"You let Chuck go, right?"

"I drove him home and stopped to get him a soda on the way to thank him for his cooperation. He said he understood and hopes we find the person responsible."

"Chuck and Doris are good people."

"They must be to let that debacle go on in their yard tonight. The vigil was nice, then it all went apocalyptic."

"Any time Elaina's involved it gets that way."

"I heard they're taking a cruise to the Bahamas for a honeymoon."

"We should call the prayer team at the new church and start praying that Elaina doesn't sink the ship somehow."

"Just do me a favor and ask my mom first. I don't want to hear any more about how my wife is trying to take over her prayer team."

"Why does she have to be so bossy? Who died and put her in charge? Oh... that was one of those times I should've thought before opening my mouth."

"Don't tell me she's default pastor now that Pastor Sonya's gone, that it's in her will or the congregation had a vote. It would be just like Irene Hayman to weasel her way into a position of knowing everything about half the town's private, religious lives."

"You do know your mother," I said. "But, no. Nothing quite so drastic. She got the board to give her the reins to the pre-school fundraising campaign since she's already given so much money to it, *but*--and here's the strange part--we have it on good authority that the board didn't approve fundraising to start. They didn't give the green light to the pre-school plans yet and wanted to see more research."

"But, Pastor Sonya was collecting money anyway. What was she doing with it?"

This was where things got tricky. If I told him what we knew, then he could use his police connections and methods to get to the answer of Blue Horizon, LLC, and why Pastor Sonya was sending money to one of their fake businesses. But the question was, would he tell me or would I still be in the dark about the tie between Orlando, Beth Billingsley, Cecelia Evans, and possibly my mom?

"That's another avenue to go down," Ben said, answering his own question.

I was off the hook for now, but we needed to get that file folder to the cops, anonymously. The information in it could be the key to unlocking this whole case.

"Will you tell me what you find out?" I asked, laying back down on my pillow.

"If you tell me what you find out," he said, sitting up and giving me the hard-eyed stare I'd given him. "Because this is for better and for worse and withholding information about a double murder case is going to make things a lot worse for you when you're behind bars in Brookville with Sheriff Reins to keep you company."

"You would never."

"I would, and you know it, so spill it."

Now I was the one searching for a lifeline. "Fine. The only other thing is that there were receipts from a place called Educational Equipment Ltd. that we don't think exists. They're owned by Blue Horizons, LLC in Orlando where Pastor Sonya and Cecelia both lived for a short time."

"Blue Horizons, LLC," Ben said, throwing the covers back and hopping out of bed. "Don't wait up. I'm going to the station to see what I can dig up."

"Tell me what you find!" I called to him as he darted out the hall with his jeans in one hand and shoes in the other.

The last body that turned up in this town, Ben and I teamed up to solve the case. I hoped this time would be the same and he wouldn't go back to his old ways to keeping me in the dark since I didn't have a badge.

I had a feeling there was more to this than what was on the surface. Money being laundered was one thing, but why did it lead to murder--two murders? Or did it have anything to do with the deaths at all?

15

Sunday morning found me at church. It was hot and sticky like fire and brimstone, but that's not the kind of church it was. The AC wasn't working and with so many people crammed into the pews in their Sunday best, the place was drowning in sweat.

We fanned ourselves with our programs and tried to pay attention while the associate pastor droned on about the future of the church leadership with Pastor Sonya gone.

Irene sat to my left with Stewart on the opposite side of her, and Mia sat on my right. I kept nudging her to put her phone away.

The service was as brief as possible to get all the required Sunday worshiping in while avoiding parishioners passing out in the pews.

Afterward, Mia and I stood with Irene and Stewart in the narthex while they mingled. There was a lot of chatter about the vigil and the wedding, which was referred to in terms like eccentric and shameful. I figured we couldn't win them all.

Irene introduced me and Mia to her friends who stopped to say hello, then go on talking like we weren't there. It was exactly what I was hoping for, unsolicited inside information.

Opal Mavis, Reverend Stroup's secretary, was there. She came up with a scowl on her face ready to gossip. "Can you believe this place calls itself a church?" she asked, obviously not realizing that Irene and Stewart were members. "Our Reverend would be beside himself. Did you hear the stuttering, fumbling recitation of Matthew 1:18? The readers need to be made to practice their readings." Then she leaned in like she had a big secret to share. "I heard from the woman sitting behind me that the church is in big financial trouble and that's why there was no air conditioning today. They can't afford it."

Irene pursed her lips and looked away. "That can't be the case."

I wondered if she was thinking about the pre-school fund and all the money she'd donated. Surely, if the church were planning on expanding into a pre-school in the next couple of years, there had to be good tithing revenue coming in.

"Irene," I said, tossing caution to the wind, "you said you were in charge of the pre-school fundraising now, right? Do you have records for that? I was just curious how money was flowing to that fund if there was nothing for air conditioning for Sunday service."

Opal's eyes widened at learning Irene wasn't just a member of the church, but in charge of something as important as fundraising. "It was nice seeing all of you," she said, and turned and stalked off.

Irene's head snapped to face me. "Why are you asking me about financial records that are none of your business?"

"I think it's a clue to what's been going on."

"Going on?"

"Pastor Sonya, and my mom's wedding planner."

"It couldn't possibly have anything to do with our pastor doing what she did."

"Ben thinks it was done *to* her. I'd like to see those records and see if they match what I've learned about her fundraising or where she was funneling the money."

"Funneling the--" She shook her head and rolled her eyes. "Cameron you have such a wild imagination. We'll go back to the house and I'll show you. There's nothing in the records to indicate that anything suspicious was going on."

Irene was so stubborn she wouldn't think a rock was hard if it hit her in the head. "Thank you," I said. "I'd like to take a look before dragging Ben into something that's just a hunch."

She was a sucker for Ben, so by bringing up his name and how I was doing it for him, she'd simmer down about it.

She took a deep breath, straightened the pink jacket of her skirt suit, and smiled. "It's very nice of you to guard his time like that. He's so busy with important work, he doesn't need to be pestered about church records."

Steward clapped a hand on Mia's shoulder. "Before we head back to the house, let's get our chicken dinners. I'm starving."

Sundays after church the Cornerstone was packed wall to wall with a line out to the parking lot. At this rate, I'd spend half my day without any progress in the case.

"I have to work in an hour, Grandpa," Mia said, saving herself from waiting for a table in a hot blacktop parking lot.

"Let's order it to go, Stewart," Irene said. "You can pick it up and we can eat it at home."

"All right," he said. "I'll drop you ladies off and head on over to the restaurant. I'll order it and wait for it."

"You'll drink a beer and watch ESPN in the bar," Irene said, smirking.

"Would I do that?" Stewart asked, and laughed. He ruffled Mia's hair like she was a little kid and led her toward the doors.

"I told him not to do that to her," Irene said, watching them. "She's going to be a senior in high school."

"She'd tell him if it bothered her." I suspected she liked being seen as a kid still by her grandpa.

We followed Stewart and Mia out of the church, and my phone rang as soon as I sat down in the backseat of the car. "It's Ben," I said, and answered. "Hi! I'm with your parents and Mia. We're just leaving church."

"Hi," he said. "I need a favor."

"Sure, what's up?"

"The officer at the gatehouse called and your mom was going bananas in the background. From what I gathered Brutus tried to go after Grace when she came to the castle. I can't imagine him going after someone for no reason. He was trained by Quinn, and nobody knows how to train K9's better than him."

"Oh, good gravy. I mean, sure, when I first met Brutus he wanted to eat me, but we were on good terms soon after."

"And that was before he had any training at all. He didn't even know the sit command."

"What do you want me to do?"

"Can you go pick him up, please? I'd go, but with these two cases I'm swamped."

"No problem. I'll get him and bring him home. Should I grab Conan too for Quinn?"

"Might as well. I think your mom's had it with all the dogs. Tell everybody hello for me."

"Will do," I said. We exchanged goodbyes and I hung up. "That was Ben, he says hello."

"What was all the fuss about?" Irene asked, making no secret of the fact that she as being nosy. I told her what happened and that I had to go pick up the dogs.

"I'll look through the financial records," Irene said. "If what Opal said was true and the church is broke, I need to take a good look at those anyway."

"Please let me know if anything looks suspicious, will you?"

"If it'll help." She turned around and smiled. It was the kind of smile that said she'd be more than happy to have me owe her something.

I DROVE up to the gate at Hilltop Castle to find Brutus in the outdoor kennel where he used to live full time before I adopted him. That was a year ago and I would've never guessed in a million years that he'd be an official officer and Ben's trusted partner.

The uniformed cop staying at the gatehouse motioned for me to roll my window down. "Hi, Mrs. Hayman," he said.

"Hi, Officer Eddie. I heard Brutus was up to his old ways again."

"I don't think so." Eddie scratched his chin. "He acted within the parameters of his training. Something tipped him off."

"Drugs? Does Grace have drugs in her car?" I was joking, but for all I knew she did.

"No, he didn't alert on the car, it was the woman."

"Well, I'm here to take him home. I'm going to go say hello to my mom and Carl first though."

"I'll get the gate."

"Thanks."

I cruised up to the house and parked by the door. Mom came rushing outside. "That dog has to go."

"I know. I'm here to take him home."

"What a nightmare! Poor Grace and all she's gone through and then to be attacked by a vicious animal!"

"She wasn't attacked. Brutus is a trained police dog. He alerted to her for a reason."

"What reason could that dog possibly have to freak out on Grace?"

"I don't know, Mom, did you ask him?"

"Did I *ask* him? Don't you get smart with me, Cameron."

When Mom lost her cool and started overreacting it made me turn into a teenager for some reason.

"I'm taking Conan, too, so you won't have them in your hair. How is Grace?"

"Come in. She's fine. Giving Leopold a bath."

"A bath? He seemed clean to me."

I followed her inside and into the kitchen where Grace had Leopold in the oversized sink filled with bubbles.

"He smelled like Pastor Sonya's perfume," Mom said. "It was ghastly."

"I thought it was okay," Grace said. "He likes baths." She dumped a plastic bowl full of water over the dog's head.

"I'm sorry about Brutus," I said. "I hope he didn't scare you too much."

"I'm okay. It was a surprise, that's for sure. I rolled down my window for the officer and the dog jumped halfway in at me."

"He must've smelled something or heard something that made him act like that."

"I don't know what. I've only been at the Briar Bird Inn."

"Maybe it was Judy's chicken and dumplings. I'd jump in a car after those, too."

"This is no joking matter, Cameron," Mom said, but Grace laughed.

"I haven't had the chicken and dumplings yet," she said, "but maybe Judy will make some before I go home. I hope Officer Hayman lets me leave soon."

"I don't know what he's found out. Has he interviewed you yet?"

"Not yet. I'm nervous about it. Why does he need to interview me?"

"He has everyone on his suspect list. Which reminds me, I need to find out where Dad was the night of both deaths. I'm not even sure he was in town yet."

"Your dad needs an alibi?" Grace's mouth dropped open. "That's brutal."

"Tell me about it. No special treatment for anybody as far as Ben's concerned."

"I got a text from your father earlier," Mom said, "inviting us over tonight for those steaks he's still planning on cooking out."

"Well, so far there's no vigil/wedding combo going on tonight and I plan on keeping it that way, so sounds good to me. Grace, come over and join us."

"Of course she will," Mom said. "If she's stuck in this little town, at least we can feed her and keep her company."

Grace draped a towel over the front of herself and lifted Leopold out of the sink, holding him to her and wrapping the ends of the towel around him. "Now you look like a baby in a blankie, yes you do," she cooed to the dog.

Leopold made sounds like he was talking to her and licked her nose.

"What a good boy," Mom said. "You can round up your animal and Quinn's and take them home now," she told me.

"You don't like Conan either?"

"He's fine. Doesn't have much personality though. We couldn't get him to play ball with Leo."

I looked into the hallway where Conan, the Irish Wolfhound, had silently taken a seat by the suit of armor. They were similar in color and stature, with broad shoulders and stiff backs. Conan was a very dignified and intelligent dog who took his duty seriously. There would be no playing the part of a house pet on his watch.

Whatever had alerted Brutus to Grace, Conan hadn't picked up on it. That led me to believe that whatever it was, Brutus had linked Grace to something or somewhere else. That K9 and I needed to spend a little time together thinking this through.

Well, he'd run around with Gus and the twins and I'd think it through. Such was the life of a police dog mom.

16

On the way home from the castle with Brutus and Conan, I noticed that the police tape was down at the old church. Reverend Stroup and Opal Mavis were on their way in the side door.

I stopped and got out of the car with both dogs. Ben wasn't around and this was my chance to look around the church with the two people who knew it best. If anything looked out of whack, they would know.

"Good Morning, Reverend Stroup," I said. "Hello, Opal, seems like I just saw you." I chuckled at my dumb joke.

"I was just telling the Reverend about how unorganized that service was over there," Opal said, still scowling. She gave both dogs a pet on their heads. "Such nicely behaved dogs. Reminds me of my Cookie. She's a husky mix, have I told you about her?"

"I've seen you in Dog Diggity with Cookie," I said. "She's a pretty girl. How's your voice Reverend?" I asked.

He only shook his head.

"The doctor says it might be gone for as long as two weeks," Opal answered for him. "And we have a baptism coming up next weekend."

"Better not let my dad hear about that. He's never done a baptism."

Reverend Stroup made a growling sound and shoved the door open.

"Do you mind if I come inside and check out the basement? I want to make sure the police didn't make a mess down there with their search for evidence."

The Action Agency typically worked down there instead of at my house, although it felt like we always ended up around my kitchen table even when the church was available.

Reverend Stroup nodded and waved me downstairs.

"We'll be around if you need us," Opal said.

I flipped on the basement lights and made my way down the stairs. The floor was black and white checked linoleum and the walls were painted-over mildew. The air was always damp and musty, and today it was humid from the church being closed up for a couple of days.

I plugged in our giant fan and cracked the basement windows open. The dogs seemed to think they were on duty and sat on either side of the steps. Nothing seemed to be amiss. Not that there was much to search. Five old school desks and a card table. Some office phones from the '80's. We had a few binders and index cards that we used for official Metamora Action Agency business, like planning Canal Days or the Winter Festival, but anything related to our sleuthing we kept with us and not in the church.

My goal wasn't to check out the basement anyway. I needed to get up in the choir loft.

I said, "Come," to the dogs, and took the steps back upstairs with both of them on my heels. We made our way down the aisle to the altar, both of them sniffing and darting back and forth like they were searching for buried treasure. They stuck their heads under the same pew that Gus had gotten his stuck underneath and gave a sharp bark. That was where I figured Leopold had been hiding.

The dogs followed as I went through the door on the right of the altar where the office was located. The office door was closed, so the Reverend and Opal wouldn't see me snooping around.

To the left a staircase rose to the choir loft. I tiptoed up with

Brutus and Conan pushing their way ahead of me. At the top I took a few steps out into the balcony where the choir sat.

"Looking for us?" Opal asked.

Startled, I jumped and almost toppled over the railing. "Good gravy, you scared me."

She and Reverend Stroup seemed to have the same idea I had. They were on their knees examining the bottom of the rail where the the rope would've been tied.

"We thought we'd come up here and make sure no damage was done to the railing," she said.

"Me, too," I stammered, which was a clear lie to all of us, even the dogs.

The canine duo took up their sniffing and darting around operation, but this time they both made an excited whining sound as they followed a path their noses dictated, ending right where Opal and the Reverend were kneeling. Then they began to bark and paw at the railing.

Reverend Stroup nodded, his brows raised in surprise. He gave Conan a pat on the shoulder and said, "Good boys," in a raspy whisper.

"They sure are good boys," Opal said, standing and brushing off her skirt.

I stepped between the dogs and got a good look at the railing, then I bent and sniffed it. I don't know what I was hoping to smell. If there had been anything detectable to the human nose, it was long gone with time and all of the police and whatever forensics they did. I didn't smell anything but the faint scent of old wood polish that everything inside the church smelled like.

Brutus and Conan definitely smelled something else though. Since I didn't know how they were trained, I couldn't be sure that what they were smelling was the same each time, or different scents and what it was about those scents that made them alert to them. They weren't trained to be cadaver dogs, so I knew they weren't reacting to the location due to it being where Pastor Sonya died. They had to be alerting to a scent they'd found before or were told to track.

"We think these are rope fibers," Opal said, pointing to a spot on the first bench where straw colored, splinters of rope lay scattered. It reminded me of pine needles that fall under the Christmas tree. "We should tell Officer Hayman," she said. "They must've missed these in their search."

"I'll tell him," I said, bending closer to get a better look.

It was hard to see the extremely small fibers, at least enough to tell if there was anything noteworthy about them.

Opal leaned her head in next to me. "We figured this must be where she sat to make the noose."

"That makes sense. Tying a knot in an old rope would leave shards of rope fibers like this."

"We think it was the rope from the custodian's closet. It had mildew and paint on it, and it was old, so it would leave splinters like this. And look here, there's a teensy purple paint chip that must've fallen off of it."

"Is the rope from the closet missing?"

"It's gone," she said.

"That must be a correct guess, then."

I straightened up and took a few steps back to get some personal space. The loft was small as it was and with the three of us and the dogs all jammed into the same couple of feet, I was feeling a bit penned in.

Hot air rises, and up in the choir loft it was blazing. I hadn't eaten anything and I couldn't remember the last sip I had to drink. Before church, surely. Dizziness overtook me, and I began to sway.

"Cameron?" Opal said, "are you okay?"

In answer, I dropped to the floor, everything going black on my way down.

When I opened my eyes again, I wasn't sure where I was. The hardwood floor underneath me didn't give me any clues. Then there were two faces looming over me.

"Reverend Stroup? Opal?" It all came rushing back. "I passed out."

"You did!" Opal fanned my face with a hymnal. "Now just lay there for a minute. Don't get up too fast or you'll end up right back down there."

I looked to my left and saw the dogs sitting beside the railing. To my right were the choir pews. Underneath, a Bible lay open. "Mathew 1:18," I said.

"Oh, I told the Reverend all about that awful reading at the new church this morning," Opal said. "Don't you worry about that. It's the only time I've heard the immaculate conception flubbed so badly."

I reached for the book and pulled it out from under the bench. "It's open to Matthew 1:18."

Reverend Stroup's brow gathered.

"That's a strange coincidence," Opal said, taking the Bible from me and closing it. "Let's get you up."

Was it a coincidence though?

~

I GOT the dogs home and was blessed with time alone. Mia was working at the Soda Pop Shop. Monica was working at Dog Diggity. Ben was doing whatever Ben did when he was working on a case.

Wait. Where was Dad?

I sent him a text message asking him where he'd gotten off to.

Soapy took me to the store. I'm buying things for the cookout tonight.

The way Dad made friends so easily, it wasn't a surprise that he could get divorced, travel the world, and end up happier than he'd ever been. He was a man who craved new experiences and new people in his life. Thinking about it now, it was amazing he and Mom stayed married for as long as they did. She was one for familiarity, family, and home, which was why she ended up following Monica here when she moved, and had ended up engaged after only a few months of living in Metamora.

I made a sandwich and got a big glass of iced tea, then sat down to think through what I knew about both cases.

In Pastor Sonya's case, the rope was from the church and it was old. It frayed and when it was tied, leaving fibers and at least one paint chip to identify it.

Leopold had been there when it happened and he didn't belong to Pastor Sonya like we thought.

The dogs alerted to scents in the church where Leopold was hiding and where Pastor Sonya was found. Brutus had found a scent outside the church the day we found Pastor Sonya. I remembered Quinn calling to Ben when he saw that the dog had found a scent trail.

So if those scents were the same, the person who was inside the church with Pastor Sonya had come in the side door we always used, had left their scent on Leopold, and had at least touched the rope that was used in the death.

The side door was used by a handful of us in town who still used the old church. Opal stopped in each morning, and she'd have reason to be there if a wedding was going to take place the next day. She liked dogs and had at least one. She could've gotten a second dog recently. She knew all about the rope just from some fibers and linked it with the missing one from the closet.

And Opal hated the new church. Reverend Stroup was cut out of the position of being the pastor there and they hired Pastor Sonya, and Opal was fiercely loyal to Reverend Stroup.

She had the motive and the access to the church and the rope. She would've had to meet Pastor Sonya at the church and lure her there, most likely due to Reverend Stroup's laryngitis. They'd need to go over Mom and Carl's ceremony the next day.

"It all fits," I said, my mind reeling. "Opal Mavis killed Pastor Sonya."

17

I should've known Dad would invite everyone he's met in Metamora to our house for his cookout. So far it was me, Mia, and Ben, of course, Monica, Quinn, Carl, Mom, Grace, Irene, Stewart, Soapy and his wife Theresa. Our family get together had turned into a party.

Then my Action Agency arrived.

"Joe told us there were steaks," Roy said.

"I brought brownies," Anna said, handing me a pan.

"Thanks. Come on in. We're out back." I led my crew through to the kitchen and got them set up with drinks on their way outside. Anna and Logan each took a bottle of water and joined the others in the backyard.

"Iced coffee for me," Roy said. "It's too daggum hot for hot coffee."

"Drink iced tea," Johnna told him.

"I need caffeine. Do you want me to backslide right off this wagon?"

"Tea has caffeine you old buffer."

"Don't start with me ya old nag."

"I have news," I said, interrupting their bickering.

"Who else died?" Roy asked.

"Nobody, but I think I figured out who killed Pastor Sonya."

Ben came in through he back door. "Welcome," he said. "It's a party now that Roy's here."

"No, no," Roy said. "I don't party anymore. I'm strictly a wagon rider."

"Good for you. That takes a lot of will power and dedication. How long has it been?"

"Too long. I'm not counting, just taking it a day at a time."

"Seven harrowing days," Johnna said. "Plus a few hours."

"Don't make it seem like you're doing the harrowing," Roy told her. "I'm the hero in this story."

"That's not what harrowing--never mind," Ben said. "Cam, do we have any more of the veggie dip?"

"Check in the fridge," I said. "I don't know what all Dad bought."

"About this news, Cameron," Roy said.

"Zip it," Johnna whispered, elbowing him.

"What news?" Ben asked.

"Oh, uh, there's a baptism next weekend and Reverend Stroup might not have his voice back," I said, improvising. "Dad might fill in if he's still in town."

Ben turned to the fridge and opened the door. "If Joe's not careful, he'll end up staying like your mom and Monica did."

In a strange way that made sense given how easily Dad had fit in here.

Ben grabbed the dip and a container of veggies. "Cam," he said, "can you take those foil packets of mushrooms and onions out to your Dad for me? I'm out of hands."

"Sure, I'll grab them." Dad was an expert griller. Everything that could be cooked on the grill grate or steamed in a folded up square of foil was fair game.

Following Ben outside with Dad's mushrooms and onions, I whispered to Roy and Johnna as I passed by them, "Later."

"Toss some ice in your coffee and let's get outside with the others," Johnna said as I stepped out onto the patio.

The dogs were running around greeting people and begging for snacks. Soapy gave Gus and Leopold carrots. Brutus and Conan were acting like regular dogs, enjoying their time off duty. Colby and Jack were glued to Dad's side, hoping for a steak. Monica and Quinn brought Isobel with them to visit her unruly fur brothers. She took her spot behind the birdbath against the garage and guarded it by growling at anyone who came within ten feet. Mia held Liam so he didn't get stepped on, and fed him chips.

Leopold made quick friends with Gus and the two of them carried a stick around the yard, one holding each end.

"Isn't this nice?" Dad said, putting an arm around me. He wore an enormous smile. "Good friends and good food. A nice summer evening. What more could you want out of life?"

"You like it here, don't you?" I asked him.

"I do like it here. It's homey, but not boring. The people are interesting, and it seems like there's always something going on. Plus, my girls are here! Even your mother."

"Do you miss Mom?"

He glanced across the yard to where Mom stood with Carl and Grace talking with Irene and Stewart. "Not in a way that would threaten what she and Carl have. I miss her like I'd miss any family member I was with for over forty years. I like her now. Like a friend. It's hard to do that when you're married and have the other pressures of a relationship coming down on you."

"You should stay for a while. Are you planning on traveling anywhere soon?"

"Not until fall. Maybe I'll hang around here a little longer if you and Ben let me."

"I think that would be okay." I hugged him. It was nice having my dad around.

~

DAD'S STEAKS WERE AMAZING. New York strips cooked to perfection. The dogs all got a steak bone and were laying in the grass chewing on their loot. Anna brought out her brownies, Irene cut a strawberry cake she made, and Soapy and Theresa served up a rhubarb pie.

We were all stuffed, and I had no idea how I'd fit dessert in, but I was going to try my darnedest.

"I need to go get some things," Dad said, getting up from the patio table. "Be right back."

"Oh no," Monica whispered beside me. "You don't think he brought presents do you?"

My dad was good at a lot of things, but picking out gifts wasn't one of them. He didn't need to get us anything, but he always did and usually stuck with money for Christmas and birthdays, especially since he'd been traveling a lot over the past year.

"You don't need coconut shell maracas?" I asked her, laughing.

"About as much as you need a snake skin head wrap."

"I'll add it to my exotic collectibles box in the attic."

"The one marked garage sale?" she asked, giggling.

Dad came back outside carrying boxes and bags. "I haven't gotten my family under one roof for five minutes since I arrived," he said. "I hope the rest of you are okay with me giving them some things I picked up on my travels."

"Absolutely," Soapy said. "I bet you have a ton of pictures to show us, too."

I groaned inwardly. I'd seen dad's pictures and they were mostly close up selfies of the side of his face and a very narrow part of the background. One he said was him in front of the Great Pyramid, but all I saw was some sand and his forehead in the picture.

Dad passed out the gifts. Monica and I each had a long, thin box. "I'm guessing we got the same thing," she said.

Ben got a small gift bag, and Dad gave Quinn a bottle of his favorite Irish whiskey. Mia got a square box wrapped in white paper.

Dad shoved his hands in his pockets. "Go ahead," Dad said, "open them."

Ben took a small, black jewelry box out of the bag and opened it. "A gold, first responders pin. How thoughtful, Joe. Thank you."

Smiling, Dad rose up on his tip toes and back down. "Got it in Bangkok. Good prices on gold over there."

Monica and I opened ours at the same time. "A silk scarf," I said. "It's very pretty."

"Mine's a different color," Monica said. "Thanks, Dad."

"Yes, thanks," I said, wrapping the scarf around my neck.

I'd never wear a silk scarf, it was too light weight for winter and too dressy for working in a church basement. It was lovely though, a definite step up from coconut shell maracas.

"Indian silk," Dad said. He pointed at Mia. "Your turn. I have to admit, it's American. I got it at the airport duty free. It seemed like you."

Mia tore off the paper. "Perfume!" She opened it and pulled out a little bottle and popped off the filagreed gold top. "It smells good," she said, spraying it on her wrist. "Like candy."

I recognized the bottle, and was sure Mia had one just like it already. "Let me see," I said.

Mia passed it over to me and I sniffed the sprayer. The scent sparked my memory. I remembered where I'd seen the bottle and where I'd smelled the scent before. I looked across the table at Grace. "You wear this, don't you?" I showed her the bottle.

Everything came rushing to me. Leopold at the church, me being in Grace's suitcase at the Briar Bird, why Brutus alerted on Grace.

I held her eyes and she blinked a few times, trying to get out from under my gaze. She knew I had her.

"Sometimes," she said. "Excuse me." She got up from the table. "May I use your bathroom?"

"I'll show you were it is," Mia offered.

I nudged Monica and she got my vague message. "I'll show her, Mia. I need to go in, too."

I waited until they were inside to stand up. "Everything was really good. Roy, do you want more iced coffee?"

"Love some," he said.

"Come show me how you like it," I said.

I quickly widened my eyes, hoping to give him a clue that I needed to talk to him.

"I'll like it however you make it," he said.

Johnna had seen my non-verbal message and got up. "Help me bring in these dishes, you old coot," she said.

"You women just won't let a man sit and relax for five-seconds will ya?" Roy got up and collected some plates.

"We'll help," Anna said, tugging Logan to his feet as she rose from her chair. "Everyone else sit and talk. We'll take care of this."

"Action Agency business in the kitchen is what I'm getting from this," Ben said.

Johnna swatted Roy. "I swear you couldn't get a secret message if it was painted in red on the side of a barn."

"Anything I need to be aware of?" Ben asked.

"Not yet," I told him.

I had to be sure the connection I was putting together in my head was real. I wan't going to make accusations to the police that wouldn't stick.

18

Roy, Johnna, Logan, and Anna gathered in the kitchen. I waved them into the dining room and closed the pocket doors.

"Is this the news you had to tell us?" Roy asked.

"It's news, but different news. At first I was certain that Opal had killed Pastor Sonya."

"Opal Mavis?" Johnna cackled. "She wouldn't eat a cracker in the church, let alone kill someone."

"I didn't think of that," I said. "But all the other pieces fit together. She hates the new church, she's loyal to Reverend Stroup and he was passed over for the job at the new church."

"That's flimsy at best," Roy said.

"She knew the rope used was from the custodian's closet."

"She would know the rope was missing though, wouldn't she?" Anna asked. "Maybe not."

I waved my hands. "None of that matters now. It wasn't her. It was Grace."

"Grace?" Johnna asked. "That little thing? How in the world would she be able to haul Pastor Sonya over a railing?"

"I don't know exactly how it happened."

"This sounds like Opal all over again," Roy said.

"Let's hear the evidence," Logan said.

"First, the dog, Leopold. He was left in the church by someone who was there with Pastor Sonya. He smelled like that perfume Mia just got. B) Brutus sniffed around the crime scene and then he alerted on Grace. Nobody knew why, but it was her perfume. Lastly, when Monica and I went to the Briar Bird to tell Grace that we found Cecelia, we helped her get cleaned up and I found that same bottle of perfume in her suitcase. Leopold is hers and he was left at the church."

"How does that tie her to the murder though?" Anna asked. "I get that she was at the church and for some reason left without her dog, but that's all it proves."

She was right. It only proved that she had been in the church and left her dog. Maybe she couldn't afford him anymore and figured a church would be a good place to leave him? I wasn't sure, but there had to be something else. "Let me think on it."

"In the meantime," Johnna said, "we better get back outside before Ben starts spying on our meetings."

Deflated, I followed my team out of the dining room. They went out to gather more dishes and I started piling them into the dishwasher.

What a disappointment. First, they poo poo'ed Opal as the killer, then they weren't excited about my proclamation about Grace and Leopold being hers.

Logan came in and sat a mixing bowl on the counter. "I looked frame by frame at the doorbell footage you sent me from Pastor Sonya's neighbor," he said. "I'm not sure if this is anything, but Chuck goes out the front door and around the other direction, toward his garage. He doesn't come back in on the recording we have. The pastor's house is the opposite direction, but it's all I noticed."

"No cars slowing down near her driveway or license plates you could get?" I asked.

He shook his head. "Nothing like that."

"Okay, well thanks for looking."

Chuck said he and Doris weren't home. She was probably already gone and he went toward his garage to leave as well. Every possible clue was turning up empty.

"Not to alarm you," Logan said, "but Monica and Grace have been upstairs in the bathroom a while."

I stopped rinsing dishes. "They have been. Surely, one of them would be back down here by now."

I grabbed the dishtowel and dried my hands. "I'll go check on them."

"I'll come, too."

We strode down the hall and up the stairs. "Monica?" I called. "Grace?"

"Try the door," Logan said.

I turned the knob and opened the door. The bathroom was empty. "Where could they be?"

We made quick work checking the bedrooms and even the attic to confirm they weren't upstairs.

"I'm texting Anna to make sure they aren't out back. Let's check the front." Logan darted down the steps and I ran after him. He threw open the front door and bolted outside. It was still light, about an hour before the sun would set. "Did Monica drive her car or come with Quinn?"

"I don't know. I don't see her car or his truck." Panic started zinging around in my stomach. "Grace would've ridden here with Mom and Carl, so she must have taken Monica in her own car."

"We have to tell Ben. You must've been right about her."

I ran as fast as I could, holding back the hysteria that threatened to push through. I shoved through the back door and yelled, "Grace is gone and took Monica."

Nobody seemed overly concerned.

"Where did they go?" Mom asked. "Did Grace need something from the store?" She cupped her mouth with her hands and whispered to me loudly, "Maybe feminine products?"

"No. You don't understand."

"Officer Hayman," Logan said, "can we speak with you inside, please?"

"Yeah." Ben got up, staring at me. He knew something was very wrong. Johnna, Roy, and Anna came inside with him.

"As soon as they were all inside and the door was closed I laid it all out for him. The perfume, Leopold, Brutus alerting on Grace, me asking her if she wore that perfume... everything. "She knows I know," I said. "And she took off with Monica."

Ben held up his hands. "Okay, hold on. Have you tried calling Monica? Maybe it was a case where she took Grace to the store for personal items and they didn't want to announce it to everyone."

"Oh, good gravy." I yanked my phone from my pocket and dialed Monica. It rang a few times. "Voicemail," I said, and hung up.

"Let's try to calm down and think about this. Grace has never shown us that she's a threat to anyone. There was no evidence to suggest that she did anything to Pastor Sonya, even if she was at the church that day."

"Just because a young, blond, tan, girl next door with her toes all polished and--oh, Jiminy Crickets! Her nail polish!" I grabbed my keys and my handbag. "We have to find them. Monica's in trouble."

"Because of nail polish?" Ben asked. "Cameron, I'm confused."

"Ben, there were rope fibers on the first pew in the choir loft and along with them was a tiny purple chip of paint. Opal figured it came off the rope since it was old and had been used for everything and had paint on it, but I just remembered that Grace had chipped lavender nail polish on the first time I met her. She was the one who tied the rope in the choir loft!"

I didn't wait for him to respond. I ran out the door only to find that my car was blocked in. "Cripes! Bees, I wish I could instruct you to fly out and find Monica right now!"

"I'll drive," Logan said, racing out behind me. Anna, Roy, and Johnna were tagging along behind him.

"Cam, don't do anything you shouldn't," Ben called to us as we raced across the front yard to Logan's car parked on the road. "I'm calling this in. We'll find her."

"Tell Quinn and Mom," I shouted back, and slid into the passenger side of Logan's old Honda.

He fired up the engine and we raced down the street. "Which way?" he asked.

"Go by the church," Roy said. "They always return to the scene of the crime."

Logan floored it one block to the church. His tires squealed to a stop. "I don't see her car."

"I'm going to check inside really fast," I said, and hopped out.

The side door was unlocked, but that didn't necessarily mean anything. Inside the lights were off. "Hello? Monica? Grace?"

There was no answer. The church was empty.

I dashed back outside and got in the car so fast I hit my head on the top of the door frame. I bit my tongue and saw stars. "Nobody," I said, holding my head.

"Next crime scene," Anna said.

"On my way." Logan zipped out of downtown and onto route fifty-two, taking us across town to Pastor Sonya's house.

My phone vibrated with a text. It was Quinn.

With your mom, dad, and Carl. Checking the castle and Briar Bird. Ben has a patrol unit dispatched.

I sent him a text back letting him know we were checking the crime scenes.

Logan turned the corner and parked on the side of the road. The crime tape was still up. Monica's car wasn't in the driveway or on the road.

"Let's look around," Anna said, and we all piled out.

I jogged around Pastor Sonya's house while Logan, Roy, and Johnna searched around Chuck and Doris's. Anna came with me. "I'm going to break in," she said, and pulled out her student ID.

"I don't want to encourage you to break in a house again, but I need to find Monica, so I'm going to pretend I don't see you."

She slid her card in the door jam and jiggled it between the knob and the lock. The door clicked and she turned the knob. "I'm in." Then the chain on the door caught. "I'm not in. The cops must've put the chain on and went out another door."

"Or Monica and Grace are inside and Grace put the chain on the door." I rubbed my aching head. "Ben has a patrol out. They'll be showing up here any second."

She reached inside and re-locked the door before pulling it shut. "Let's see if we can look in any windows."

Just then there was a blood curdling scream coming from Chuck and Doris's yard. "That was Johnna," I said, and took off running.

Anna was in front of me in seconds. When she reached the back yard of Chuck and Doris's house, Roy ran toward her with his hands held out. "Stop! Snake!"

"I'm not afraid of snakes. There are no poisonous snakes in Indiana."

"Listen, Miss Smarty Pants, that there's a King Cobra and it's not from the wild."

"A King Cobra? Where's Logan? Did Johnna get bit?"

I came panting up to them. "Whose is it?"

"Chuck's. He said it escaped."

"It'll be dusk soon. The last thing we need is to be roaming around in a yard with a King Cobra after dark."

"We know right where it is," Roy said. "That's the trouble of it. It has Johnna cornered in the shed."

"Smoke and bones!" Anna said. "We have to get her out of there!"

"That's not all," Roy said. "The shed is like a snake house with a bunch of 'em in tanks. Let's just say I found Grace and Monica and Monica's in more trouble than Johnna."

I yanked my phone out and called Ben. "Chuck and Doris's house, fast! Monica and Johnna are in trouble with poisonous snakes. Lots of them. Hurry!"

I hung up and darted to the shed. Chuck stood outside, peering in through a crack. "This is bad," he said.

"Do you have one of those long hook things you could pick him up with?" I asked. "Get in and stick him in a bag or a bucket?"

"Not when he's like this. If anyone gets close he'll strike."

I peered in through the crack. Johnna was perched up on an overturned five-gallon bucket in the corner with the snake arched up, hood out, ready to strike. "Where's Monica?"

"Back of the shed. That crazy girl from LA has her back there, threatening to stick her hand in the viper's tank."

"Why in heaven's name do you have these things?"

He shrugged. "I like them. They're God's creatures, too."

"And he didn't put them in Indiana for a reason!"

"Get back!" Johnna shouted at the snake. "I've got a bag of yarn and I'm not afraid to use it!"

"Don't be a ninny-hammer, Johnna," Roy yelled. "Stay put and don't move!"

Sirens sounded in the distance. My heart pounded in my throat. From the back of the shed, someone was knocking on one of the glass tanks. That would agitate the snake inside.

Grace didn't know the world of hurt she'd be in if she laid one hand on Monica. I was the only one allowed to pick on my sister!

19

A SWAT team, or what passed for one in Metamora, stormed Doris and Chuck's back yard. Their flashlights swiping left and right across the yard made me feel like I was in one of those drug raids on T.V. I had no idea a tactical team of law enforcers could be assembled so fast in our little corner of the state. A few of them had Animal Control Officer emblazoned in highlighter yellow on the back of their black shirts.

"Everybody back!" The lead officer shouted, while a few others ushered us backward.

I wanted to protest. Monica and Johnna were inside that shed, after all. But, being cuffed and tossed in a police vehicle wouldn't help anything, and these guys didn't look like they'd give me the benefit of the doubt like Ben and Sheriff Reins.

Roy, Logan, Anna, and I huddled together. Anna paced and bit her nails. Logan, who had been unnaturally heroic and take-charge, seemed to deflate, like all of the adrenaline that had gotten him this far had run out and his gas light was on. Roy was shaking.

"Roy? How you doing, buddy?" I asked. I knew if there was any time he'd want to take a drink from his flask, this was it.

"She's gotta come out of this," he said, his voice trembling. "I can't do it without her."

"She will," I said, putting an arm around his shoulders. All of his bluster and bravado fell away. Roy really cared about Johnna. I always knew they were close, but my heart ached seeing him this way.

"I'm afraid, too," I said. "My sister's in there. Johnna's in there. I have to believe they'll be okay."

The Animal Control Officers eased the shed door open. "Ma'am, please be still," they were telling Johnna. "Ma'am, don't! Ma'am!"

"Johnna, you old biddy! Don't move!" Roy yelled, and took off toward the shed.

"Roy, stop!" Anna called.

Roy ran into the fray, colliding with two officers who promptly tackled and pinned him on the ground.

"I got him!" Johnna shouted, running out of the shed holding the top of her tote cinched closed. "I tossed my knitting bag over his head and scooped him up!"

One of the Animal Control Officers rushed forward and gingerly took the wriggling bag out of her hands.

"Roy, what in tarnation are you doing on the ground?" she asked.

The officers let Roy stand back up and he shook his head. "Woman, you will be the death of me. Mark my words."

Ben and Sheriff Reins strode into the circle of officers. "Thanks for your fast response and control of the situation," Reins told the lead officer of the first responder team. "We'll take it from here."

The SWAT-like team dispersed, taking the snake with them. Ben approached Chuck and I could tell by the surly look on my husband's face that it was going to be a bad conversation for the snake owner. "Charles Abbington, you're under arrest for involuntary manslaughter in the death of Cecilia Evans. You're also being charged with owning multiple venomous snakes without a permit."

I gasped, my head fell forward, and my mouth dropped open. Chuck killed Cecelia?

Inside the shed, Grace must've had the same reaction. She

charged through the door and ran right for Chuck. *"You killed her? How could you? What did you do to her?"*

Ben let go of Chuck and grasped Grace by her shoulders. "His snake bit her. I'm going to guess that it's been loose for a while, is that right Mr. Abbington?"

Chuck shuffled his feet. "He got out a few weeks ago. I searched and searched. I thought he was probably long gone by now. I had no idea that's what happened to that poor woman." His face was scrunched, fighting emotions. He was pained to hear his carelessness had caused Cecelia's death.

"We've been checking every registered snake owner in a fifty-mile radius," Sheriff Reins said "We're lucky it came to this tonight or we might've never caught you."

Reins escorted Chuck out of the back yard toward the squad car, while reading him his rights.

Monica ambled out of the shed looking like she'd stumbled out of a nightmare. I ran to her and grabbed her in a bear hug. "Thank God you're okay."

"I hate snakes," she said, and started crying.

"I can't believe that's how Cecelia died. I wonder if the snake bit her in the house or outside?"

"The snake isn't talking," Roy said. "Monica I'm happy to see you out of that shed with no puncture holes in ya."

Monica wiped her eyes and sniffled. "I just want to go home."

"Let me drive you," Roy said. "Johnna, dear, let's take this young lady and her car home. We'll pick up your car and you can follow us out to her house."

"Always telling me what to do," Johnna grumbled, but when she whacked him in the arm it was soft and with a grin.

Monica didn't make it two steps before Quinn came sprinting through the yard and swooped her off of her feet into his arms.

"Guess she don't need a ride," Roy said, then he turned to me. "Think we can stop for coffee on the way home?"

~

Based on my information, Ben had one of the Brookville officers collect the rope fragments and purple paint chip from the pew in the choir loft. He took Grace into custody for questioning and held her while they ran tests on her nail polish and the paint chip.

I knew they had the right person, but Mom wasn't convinced. "Do you think Cecelia would hire a murderer?"

We were sitting in her dining room the next day looking at wedding invitations--again. They were thinking about a Christmas wedding this time, at the castle so nobody would have the opportunity to *compromise* their big day.

I didn't tell Mom, but in my experience the venue didn't matter much. When murder was in the air in Metamora, it wasn't kind enough to plan it around your wedding location. I kept hoping it wouldn't happen again, but it seemed to be on a tear in our town.

"I don't understand her motive," Monica said. "Why would she want to kill a woman she's never met?"

"She didn't!" Mom said. "So what if Leopold is her dog, *if* he turns out to be. That only means she stopped to check on the church and probably to look for Cecelia when she got to town. That's what she gets paid to do. It was her whole reason for being here."

"No, there was something funny going on with the pre-school fundraising and money going to places in Orlando. Cecelia and Pastor Sonya were connected, you know that, they were both your sorority sisters."

"And hadn't seen one another for years, Cameron." Mom sighed, exasperated.

"That doesn't explain how Cecelia ended up in Pastor Sonya's house with a file of financial information."

Mom shook her head, looking like she'd sucked on a lemon. "Well, I just don't know how that could be."

Leave it to Mom to refute facts if they didn't fit into her narrative. "Anyway," I said. "Ben will figure it out."

"I don't think I've ever heard you say that," Monica said.

I thought it was obvious that Mom was the only reason I was dropping the subject. Of course I wasn't going to just leave it to him. If the paint matched that would prove it, but I wanted to figure out the why. What was Grace's motive? How did she factor into what was at play between Cecelia and Pastor Sonya?

"Well, I've learned my lesson," Monica said, "and I promised Quinn I wouldn't stick my nose into any more police business. I'm sticking it in my own business, Dog Diggity."

"Very smart move," Mom said. "I hate to think about what could've happened to you in that snake pit."

"It was a shed," I said.

Mom blinked at me in dismay. "Does that make it any better? Any less dangerous?"

I looked down to the bridal magazine I'd been assigned and flipped through the pages. When Mom and Monica got overdramatic the best thing for me to do was to check out of the conversation.

I wasn't dismissing Monica's experience in the shed, and a viper bite could've been critical if not fatal, like Cecelia. Although, Cecelia had been ill to begin with. Monica would've gotten an antidote immediately. But next thing you knew, Mom would be saying Monica was almost sacrificed to the Mayan serpent God, Kukulkan. I'd been down this road before and bought the t-shirt.

Then there was the bomb that Monica dropped, saying she wouldn't be involved in anymore sleuthing. I don't know why it bothered me so much. I didn't even want there to be any more sleuthing to do, but if something did crop up, I was left with Roy and Johnna. Logan and Anna were leaving in a few weeks for college, so the Action Agency would be down to me and the two squabbling senior citizens. They were good partners, if only they could stop bickering for two-seconds.

I closed my eyes and yawned. With the wedding planning and then the murders, maybe I just needed a nap.

20

I woke up when Mia and Dad came barging into the house like a herd of mad cows singing a Taylor Swift song at the top of their lungs. The dogs ran around barking, joining in on the impromptu party happening.

"What are you doing sleeping?" Dad asked. "It's four in the afternoon." He plopped down in the chair in the corner of the living room. Gus set his head on Dad's leg for pets.

Mia's footsteps ran up the stairs and into her room. "Liam!" she called. "Come on, fuzzbum!" Liam pitter-patted across the kitchen and up the steps, then the bedroom door closed.

"I know teens rarely leave their bedrooms, but I'm still amazed at how much time she spends in there."

"You were the same way. You and Monica. You'd come out long enough to eat us nearly broke then hide yourselves back in there."

"Good to know my eating habits haven't changed. Where were you two?"

"We drove up to the Muncie Mall."

"That's over an hour away."

"A grandpa and his granddaughter on summer vacation have all the time in the world. We ate hot pretzels and drank slushies, saw a terrible movie, and I bought her a new shirt."

"Wow, Dad, that sounds like a lot of fun."

"You want me to take you tomorrow?"

"Maybe we should rummage around some of the shops here in town. You haven't been to many of them yet."

"That's true. Plus you want to stay close to hear if that Grace is charged." He winked.

"Ben would call and tell me."

"You'd hear it first through the grapevine, and you can't tell me any different."

"Okay, you got me. I'm still hoping to hear something today though."

"Nah, they had to send those samples to the lab. They'll have the results back tomorrow since he's got her on a forty-eight hour hold."

"How do you know?"

"Don't you ever watch true crime shows?"

My Dad. World traveler, ordained minister, true crime junkie.

"I should figure out what we're having for dinner." I stood from the couch and stretched.

"Pizza," Dad said. "I'm ordering. You've had a long weekend. Sit back down and relax."

I did as I was told and Colby and Jack grumbled about sharing the couch again.

Dad looked up a place in Brookville on his phone that delivered and called to order. "The works?" he asked.

I nodded, and yawned again. It was nice having my Dad around to take care of things, even if he did do it his own way and sometimes with questionable methods.

The doorbell rang. The dogs barked and took off down the hall. "I'll get it," Dad said. Pushing himself up out of the chair.

I heard the door open and dad say, "You're not the pizza guy," and laugh.

"You ordered a pizza?" I heard Roy ask. "Then we're just in time."

"You just ate," Johnna said. "I swear that flask of yours used to fill a hollow leg."

"Hi guys," I said, when they got to where I could see them in the kitchen. "What's going on?"

"Did we interrupt your afternoon bonbons?" Roy asked.

"Shut up, Roy," Johnna said. "Cameron, we think we're on to something with Pastor Sonya, but we need Logan and his computer."

"Yeah," Roy said. "We know she has a daughter who Elaina says is still in Orlando. She says her name is Sarah. We wondered if we could check that out on that family page thingie Logan searched on before."

"Ancestry dot com," I said. "I can search on my phone. Let me bring up the website."

"Your phone?" Johnna said. She took her ancient flip phone out of her knitting bag and stared at it. "Does mine do that?"

"I don't think so. It has to be a smartphone."

Roy cackled. "Your phone's dumb."

I pulled up the website and logged in. I'd done a lot of research on my own family tree and some on Ben's. I searched for Beth Billingsley and found the right one in Cincinnati, Sonya Beth Billingsley.

"Okay," I said. "I found her. What am I looking for?"

They hurried into the living room and sat on either side of me, squishing in to view my phone. Johnna poked at the bottom of the screen. "I want to see down there," she said.

I scrolled down. "There she is!" Roy said.

"Well, dog my cats," Johnna said. "We were right!"

They jumped off the couch laughing like hyenas, and gave each other an awkward high five, only connecting about a third of their palms.

"Hey! Remember me? Will someone tell me what's going on?"

Dad waved from the corner chair. "Me, too. I want to know."

"The middle name," Roy said, pointing to my phone.

"Sonya Beth goes by her middle name, " Johnna said, sitting back down on the edge of the couch. "Her mother's name was Betty

Virginia. On a hunch, we called the newspapers in Cincinnati to get her obituary. We found out she went by Ginny."

"It's middle names," Roy said, still jabbing his finger toward my phone. "Her daughter's name is Sarah Grace."

"Grace," I said. "Grace was Pastor Sonya's daughter?" I studied the family tree. "She had her daughter in her forties."

"When she lived in Orlando," Johnna said. "She wasn't married. I know that's not a big thing now-a-days, but for a female pastor, especially in the South it would've been a reason to lose her job."

"That's awful. So if she didn't lose her job then--"

"Then nobody knew," Roy said.

"I wonder if Grace even knew who her mother was. It's listed on this website, so it couldn't have been a secret her whole life. It's entered as a biological relation without any information about her being given up for adoption."

"When was all of that information wrote on that page, though?" Roy asked. "If it was only a year or so ago, maybe that's when Grace found out her mom was Pastor Grace."

"Where's Grace been all this time, then?" Johnna asked.

"Orlando," I said, and laughed. "That's the connection to Orlando for Pastor Sonya and Cecelia. Grace was with her mother's sorority sister, of course."

"I thought they weren't close," Johnna said, shrugging a hand in the air. "Now you want me to believe the wedding planner raised the pastor's kid?"

"What if Cecelia was looking for something related to Grace in the pastor's house?" I said. "What if she was looking for her birth certificate or searching for Grace's father's name?"

"And Grace found out and snapped?" Roy asked. "Killed her own blood?"

"If she was upset about being abandoned and left with another woman to raise her? Maybe. I don't know."

"If the paint chip fits, you can't acquit," Dad said. "This is all for nothing if Ben comes back and says the lab didn't match up the paint samples. But if they match, that's a motive if I've ever heard one. I've seen this before on Investigation Discovery. Most murders are committed by family or someone close to the victim, did you know that?"

"We've been learnin' that first hand," Roy said. "I'm startin' to think being hermit and livin' in a cave isn't a bad choice."

"Who would you harass if you lived in a cave?" Johnna asked.

"I'd send you smoke signals, old lady." He grinned and patted the top of her head, and she swatted his hand away.

"Let's get going," she said. "Ginger and my Charlie need to be walked."

Ginger was Roy's adopted Chow Chow and Charlie was a retired racing Greyhound.

They said bye to Dad and started toward the hallway. "Let us know about the paint, Cameron Cripps Hayman," Roy said.

"Will do, Roy."

The doorbell rang again and the dogs started their merry barking and tail wagging while racing to see who could get to the door faster.

"Pizza's here!" Roy called.

Dad and I followed to the door, me herding dogs so they didn't get out, but Roy and Johnna could, and Dad paying for the pizza.

"Take a piece for the road," Dad told Roy, opening the box.

"Don't mind if I do." Roy pulled a piece out, dropping half of the toppings on the floor, which Gus suctioned up like a Hoover.

We got the door closed and the pizza in the kitchen and the dogs settled back down. "What do you think about Cecelia raising Grace?" Dad asked, putting pizza on a plate. "How would she hide that all of those years? Your mother didn't know anything about it, that's for certain."

"You don't think she ever suspected? She seems overly protective of Grace. I honestly think she believes she's innocent, but I wouldn't be shocked to find out that she had an inkling about Cecelia being more than Grace's boss."

"Your mother's a mysterious woman. I always thought I knew her, then she'd turn around and do something completely out of character. Or maybe it wasn't out of character and I just never really knew her."

"Maybe she changed and you didn't notice. People do that, and you two were together a long time."

"Yeah, I'm not great at paying attention to details," he said, dripping sauce down his shirt.

"Dad," I said, pointing to the mess. "You've got something on you."

He looked down. "I did that on purpose. I like it there." He took another bite and left the sauce on his shirt.

"I guess that's your prerogative."

"Darn right it is, and I'm having donuts and bacon for breakfast."

Ah, the life of a single, retired man with nobody to answer to but himself. "Just don't tell Ben. I don't want him having any grand ideas about his prerogatives around here."

21

Ben came home that night around eleven PM. I was in bed reading, not tired after my afternoon snooze. Dad was asleep, I could hear him snoring from the guest room, and Mia was in her room, but probably not sleeping.

"Another long day," I said. "Did you have dinner? There's a couple pieces of pizza downstairs if you're hungry."

"We got pizza at the station, too." He kicked off his shoes in the closet, sat on the end of the bed and let out a long breath. "I'm beat."

"At least one case is closed, huh?" I asked, referring to Cecelia, and hoping he'd volunteer information about Grace.

"And another one darn close," he said.

"Did the lab report come back?"

He looked back over his shoulder at me. "I should have it by nine tomorrow morning."

"Dad and I are going for breakfast in the morning if you want to come along."

"You just want to be glued to my side when that call comes in."

"Will you tell me what the results are, or am I going to have to find out through the rumor mill?"

"I'll tell you, but I think we both know what it's going to say."

"Did she tell you anything today?"

He shook his head. "But it wasn't hard to find out who she really is." He watched my face for signs that I'd put this part of the puzzle together already.

"Sure," I said, "it's easy when you have her driver's license and social security number."

He laughed. "My guess is Grace found out her mother was here and confronted her."

"We're on the same path," I said.

"How'd you find out?"

"Ancestry dot com."

"Aren't you crafty."

"No, Roy and Johnna are, actually."

"You're kidding me."

"Nope. They came over tonight to tell me."

"I'm impressed."

"We're experts at this solving murders stuff now, unfortunately."

He changed into his pj's and climbed into bed. "When do Logan and Anna leave for college?"

"Two weeks, I think. Logan really came out of his shell last night with the whole Monica debacle. He took control of the situation and didn't get hives or pass out or anything."

"He's ready to go out in the world on his own," Ben said. "I can't believe Mia will be in their shoes next year."

"I can't think about that," I said. "I'm having enough trouble letting go of two who aren't family."

"I'm sure there's a couple more kids who'd like volunteer hours working for the town that you can wrangle into helping the Action Agency. With real town planning work, I mean, not the amateur cop routine."

"I'm sure there is."

But they wouldn't be my fiery, red-haired Anna, or my robot-boy Logan. I knew they'd go off and do great things someday, but letting go was hard, especially when I knew coming back to Metamora would be impossible for them if they wanted to have careers in their fields.

"Is your mom going to keep Leopold?" Ben asked.

"I'm sure she will. He'll be the crown prince of Hilltop Castle."

"That's good news for Monica. I'm sure your mom will be in Dog Diggity every day buying him toys and treats, and Johnna's dog sweaters. He'll have a bigger wardrobe than me."

I put my bookmark in my book, set it on nightstand and turned my lamp off. "I don't mind if you want to have donuts and bacon for breakfast. It's your prerogative."

"Umm... Okay. Thanks."

"But if you ever feel the need to leave spilled food on your shirt, we'll have a problem."

"Why would I do that?"

I sighed. "It's a long story."

~

DAD WAS up with the roosters banging around in the kitchen and whistling.

"I want a divorce from him, too," Ben said. "His snoring kept me up all night and now this."

I hit him in the head with my pillow. "I know he can be annoying, but he's hardly ever around."

Ben rolled over and stuffed my pillow over his head. I got up and shoved my feet in my slippers. I was too anxious to sleep anyway. It was five-thirty in the morning. Three and a half more hours until the lab called with the results.

I traipsed down the steps, hoping Dad let the dogs outside since he'd woken them up. Spook sat on the bottom stair step. "Hello again, friend," I said, bending down to pet him. "Black cats are supposed to be bad omens. I'm not sure what that means in this case."

"That's a bunch of superstitious hogwash," Dad called from the kitchen. "In Japan a black cat is good luck, did you know that?"

"Too bad we're not in Japan, then," I said, shuffling to the kitchen.

"Didn't sleep last night?" Dad asked, taking a look at me and cocking an eyebrow.

"What gave it away?"

"The big dark bags under your eyes." He poured me a cup of coffee. "Here, drink this."

I sat down at the table with my steaming brew. "Why are you up so early?"

"I travel so much that I never get acclimated to different time-zones. I only sleep four or five hours a night. Plus, that doggone CPAP machine drives me nuts and I end up pulling it off in my sleep."

At least he knew he had a snoring problem.

The dogs ran around outside in the backyard. Brutus sat on the patio looking up at the squirrels in the tree. When I first brought him home he tried to climb that tree to get a cat. He was a beast, now he was an officer. It seemed like everybody around me was growing up and changing, even the dogs.

22

Ben came tromping down the steps at a quarter till seven.

"I was going to wake you in a few minutes," I said. "Want some coffee."

"No, and you have to get dressed. We need to get to the station in Brookville."

"What? Why? What did *I* do?"

"Nothing. Grace is asking for us. *Both* of us."

"She's asking for me, too?" I jumped up from the table where I was enjoying my second cup of coffee and ran down the hall and up the stairs.

"I'm leaving in fifteen minutes," Ben yelled up after me.

That meant I had time to wash my face, brush my teeth, pull my hair into a ponytail, throw on jeans and a sweatshirt and shove my feet in my running shoes.

I tied my shoes and checked the time. Five minutes to spare. I sent a text to our Action Agency group chat to fill them in on this new development.

Roy sent back:

Can't ya put us on speaker phone in your pocket?

Johnna sent:

Yeah, if your phone's so smart it can tell us what's goin on.

Anna:

That's not what smartphone means.

Logan:

I'll try to hack into the station's surveillance cameras.

I didn't have time to argue with them or stop Logan from potentially committing a federal crime. I jogged downstairs and stood by the front door. "What's the holdup, Hayman?" I called.

"I'm coming." He strode down the hall toward me, smirking, Brutus by his side. "You're loving every second of this."

"I am." I opened the door and darted out to his police truck, Metamora One. "It's almost like I'm official now. Like we're partners," I said, climbing up in the cab and sitting beside Brutus who was parked in the middle of the seat.

"It's nothing like that." He started the truck and backed out. "Brutus is my partner."

Brutus barked in agreement.

"You two are a hard duo to break into."

We got to Brookville PD in about ten minutes. I almost asked him to go through McDonald's for an Egg McMuffin since I missed breakfast, but thought better of it. We were on professional police business.

Inside, I followed Ben past a small room of cubicles, a couple offices, and down a hall to an interview room on the right. Grace was already inside seated at the table with an officer, waiting on us.

"Hi, Grace," I said. "Or should I call you Sarah?"

I heard Ben choke a little and decided I should probably let him do the talking.

"Hi, Cameron," she said. "Officer Hayman."

We sat down at the table and the other officer left the room, closing the door behind him.

"Why did you ask to see us this morning?" Ben asked.

"Because I know the lab results will come back as a match," she said, "but I didn't kill Pastor Sonya."

"Do you want to tell us what happened?"

Grace rubbed her forehead and her eyes teared up. "I found out she was my mother. Cecelia raised me. I knew she wasn't my real mom. I didn't call her mom, I called her Cecelia. She always told me my mom was a friend and that someday she'd come back for me. She never did."

I opened my mouth to ask a question, and Ben stepped on my foot under the table.

"I found out last year when I took one of those DNA tests. I have a whole family I don't know. I found out who my mom was and where she was and then Angela was getting married and Cecelia was planning the wedding. I was her assistant, but more like her daughter. She didn't want me coming to Metamora. My mother, Pastor Sonya, didn't want to meet me. Didn't want anyone to find out about me. I came anyway. Cecelia was probably already dead when I got to town."

Ben waited a few beats for her to stay more. When she didn't, he prompted her. "So you stopped by the church when you got here?"

She nodded. "I didn't know my mother would be there. I wanted to see where the wedding was going to be held. I couldn't hide from Cecelia in a town this small, so I figured I'd better be some help to her. But my mother was inside."

"What happened?" I asked, completely intrigued. This was better than a Hallmark mystery.

"I asked her if her name was Beth Billingsley. She took one look at me and knew who I was." Tears fell down Grace's cheeks. "She had no interest in knowing me. She was afraid that people would find out she was a single woman with a daughter who was never married and it would turn her congregation against her. She asked if I knew how hard it was being a female in a religious profession. She said the only really accepted position for a female was being a nun, and she had to fight every day to keep her position and she wasn't going to lose it because I showed up on her doorstep."

"Matthew 1:18," I whispered. "I'm sorry," I said. "That had to be terrible to hear."

Grace whimpered. "It was. But I wouldn't let her deny me. We got into an argument."

"What kind of argument?" Ben asked. "Verbal? Physical?"

"Verbal," she said. "Across the church. I let it all out. Really told her how I felt about her leaving me and what she could do with her precious job. She told me I was killing her by showing up, that she would rather be dead than have everyone think she was an immoral woman trying to be holier than thou with some perfect life. I told her that her lies weren't my problem."

"Then what happened?" I asked.

"She got the rope out of the closet and said I should just go ahead and strangle her with it since that's what I was doing to her by being there."

"Wow," I breathed. I couldn't imagine anyone behaving that way, let alone a pastor.

"I told her if she wanted to die she'd have to do it herself, because I wasn't the one killing her. She took the rope and stormed up to the choir loft. I chased after her, afraid of what she might do, but more angry that she was being so irrational and losing her mind. I told her I'd waited my whole life for her to come back and get me, that Cecelia said she'd be back, and she never came."

"She told me Cecelia was a liar and she should've told me my mother was dead. Then she gave me an ultimatum, to leave or to watch her hang herself, because she wasn't going to just watch her life go up in flames because I strolled into her town."

Grace took a shaky sip of water.

"She threw me the rope," she said. "I called her bluff. I tied the knot and threw it back, and she... she wasn't bluffing."

Grace laid her head on her arms and sobbed. "I just wanted to know my mother."

I looked at Ben. He looked at me. Neither one of us could believe what we'd just heard. Was it the truth? It seemed genuine and convincing. On the other hand, if she knew the lab test was coming back positive, she might have made up a good cover story.

"Grace," Ben said, "thank you for telling us that story. I'm going to need you to make a formal, written statement and take a polygraph test."

"Am I still under arrest?" she asked.

"Yes," he said. "I'm holding you until the lab tests are confirmed, like you said they would be, then I'll decide the charges to file and you can call an attorney if you'd like."

She nodded and wiped at her tears, although they kept falling.

Ben stood and took my arm, helping me up. We left the room, and the officer who'd been inside when we arrived went back in to get Grace.

"If she passes the polygraph will that prove her innocence?" I asked.

"No. Polygraphs aren't permissible in court, but it'll give me a jumping off point."

"What do you mean? If she passes, she's telling the truth, right?"

"Not necessarily. Maybe a version of it. We might be looking at assisted suicide."

"What?"

"She tied the knot."

"She called her bluff."

"The pastor wasn't bluffing."

"Grace didn't know that."

"It will ultimately be up to the DA if he wants to charge her and have a trial. We present the evidence and they make that determination."

It wasn't the clear cut resolution I'd been hoping for. It wasn't the kind I'd become accustomed to. Find the bad guy, prove he did it, the end. This was going to take a lot of behind the scenes finagling and red tape before it was over.

THE ACTION AGENCY wasn't happy with the outcome either. I'd called them all together later that day at the Soapy Savant to buy them lunch for a job well done.

"A snake bite and secret daughter," Roy said, and sighed. "What happened to the days of ice picks and andirons? Murder weapons, solid evidence, and a conviction?"

"Maybe they'll let you exterminate the snake if you ask nicely," Anna said, rolling her eyes.

"That snake and all the rest are going to the zoo," Johnna said. "I called and asked."

"That's a good future for them," I said. "Better than a shed at least."

"We owe Old Dan and Elaina big," Roy said. "If it wasn't for that wedding and Elaina being able to wheedle private information out of people, like the fact that Pastor Sonya had a daughter, we'd still be spinnin' our wheels."

"I wonder why she told Elaina that when she was so determined to keep it a secret and even killed herself over it?" I asked.

"Makes me wonder if that's what really happened," Johnna said.

"Ben said she passed the polygraph."

"Polygraphs are unreliable," Logan said. "Professionals can't even agree on the accuracy and rate it somewhere between seventy and ninety percent. Results aren't allowed in trials."

"So she might be lying," Anna said.

Johnna wrapped her yarn around her needle. "She'll face the judge in the end," she said. "And He doesn't need a polygraph."

"Amen," Roy said, and took a big bite of his ham and cheese sandwich.

"You guys have to promise us something," Anna said.

"I don't have to promise nothin'," Roy said with his mouth full.

"What is it?" I asked.

She glanced over at Logan. "We want to stay in the Action Agency group text. We can help through email and phone calls, video calls. Logan does all of his work on his laptop anyway, so I figured we can still help when things come up."

"You'll be so busy with classes and college life," I said. "You aren't going to want to be texting with the three of us."

"Just promise," she said.

Johnna's face softened. "We'd never kick you kids out."

"Speak for yourself," Roy said. "These two in college are going to be insufferable."

"You used that word right," Anna said. "Good job."

"Insufferable," he said again, scowling at her.

I knew they wanted to hold on to something, a lifeline to Metamora maybe, when their whole world was changing. They were moving away, going somewhere they didn't know anyone, taking classes at a new school. We'd keep in touch with our young ones and make sure they knew we still had their backs.

This summer was a season of change, and in Metamora, that didn't happen too often. It would be nice to settle back into a state of same old same old, day after day.

At least until I stumbled onto another body.

THE SERIES CONTINUES WITH A DOG DAY'S NIGHT!

When a motorcycle club rolls into town and the leader opens a biker bar, it stirs up more than dust in Metamora.

The little canal town is known for its grist mill, antique shops, and bed and breakfasts, not for hosting a parade of noisy motorcycles. Cameron Cripps Hayman's neighbors are up in arms about the Night Hounds Motorcycle Club and even start a petition to get the mayor to ban the new establishment. But the mayor says he doesn't have the power to kick a business owner out and there's nothing in the town statutes against opening a bar.

When the Night Hound's leader is run off the road and left for dead, his wife comes to Cam and her Action Agency to track down the hit and run suspect. With her team down to two members, will they be able to solve the case as they've always done in the past? They'll give it their best rip-roaring try!

ALSO BY JAMIE BLAIR

The Deadly Dog Days Series

Deadly Dog Days

Canal Days Calamity

Fatal Festival Days

Trash Day Tragedy

Woeful Wedding Day

A Dog Day's Night

Hearing Day Homicide

Young Adult and New Adult Novels

Leap of Faith

Lost To Me

Burning Georgia

Kiss Kill Love Him Still - Series Box Set